# CASTLES AND ROSES

Kate is happy with her life as she wanders the countryside painting wild flowers for fun, and inn signs for money. Then she meets Roly, an old flame from her college days, who is living on a canal boat, and things begin to change. Fearful that her heart is becoming engaged against her will, Kate goes back to the road. It is not until after many adventures that she begins to come to terms with her need for love.

# ANDROMEDA JONES

◆

# CASTLES AND ROSES

*Complete and Unabridged*

# LINFORD
*Leicester*

First published in Great Britain in 1991 by
Robert Hale Limited
London

First Linford Edition
published 1999
by arrangement with
Robert Hale Limited
London

The right of Andromeda Jones to be identified
as the author of this work has been asserted
by her in accordance with the
Copyright, Designs and Patents Act, 1988

British Library CIP Data

Jones, Andromeda
    Castles and roses.—Large print ed.—
Linford romance library
    1. Love stories
    2. Large type books
    I. Title
    823.9′14 [F]

    ISBN 0–7089–5578–9

Published by
F. A. Thorpe (Publishing) Ltd.
Anstey, Leicestershire

Set by Words & Graphics Ltd.
Anstey, Leicestershire
Printed and bound in Great Britain by
T. J. International Ltd., Padstow, Cornwall

This book is printed on acid-free paper

To Paddy
With Love

'Twas twilight, and I bade you go,
But still you held me fast:
It was the time of roses —
We plucked them as we passed . . .

*It was the Time of Roses,*
Thomas Hood

# 1

'This is the life,' said Kate Trevine, as she swung down the lane on a bright May morning, 'free, untrammelled and independent.'

Horse chestnuts held up creamy candle-flowers above her head, there were bluebells on the banks and the dainty white stars of stitchwort. A chaffinch chanted from the hawthorn hedge, and the air smelled sweetly of wet grass after a recent shower.

Dressed in green anorak and blue jeans, with trainers on her feet, Kate stepped briskly along. If there was a seed of loneliness deep in her heart she did not think of it. In her back-pack she carried a few clothes, painting materials, a bread roll and a hunk of cheese. She was looking for the canal.

By the time she came out on to the quay the grey stones had already dried in the spring sunshine. Alongside lay a converted narrow boat, painted deep green and embellished with a gold line. Vivid bunches of ornate roses flanked the letters of her name, 'Rose Ann.' Across the water, willows touched their new leaves to the surface where a proud mallard led her brood of fluffy ducklings. It was a peaceful scene.

Dumping her pack on the ground Kate perched herself on an iron bollard to gaze. The long open hold for transporting cargo had been covered to provide extra accommodation. But the well still held the huge rudder and there was elaborate decoration on the doors leading down into the original cabin.

With a sigh of contentment Kate reached into a pocket for her sketch book and began to draw.

'Kate! You angel! What are you doing here?'

'Roly!'

Kate dropped pencil and pad as she

jumped to her feet. A large young man had surged up from the cabin, followed by an equally large woolly dog. Both gave the impression of being soft and brown and furry, though the human had light blue eyes and wore a navy-blue sweater while the dog had lambent golden eyes and wore only a battered leather collar.

In a moment Kate was swept off the ground. An untidy beard brushed her cheek. The familiar feel of his arms around her, the scent of him (compounded now with engine oil) flung her back in time.

She supposed that if she had been born with brown hair and brown eyes she would have been allowed to remain Katherine. But red hair and green eyes, and the temperament to go with them, had provoked the inevitable abbreviation. Ever since art school she had thought of herself as Kate.

In her first year at college she had been bowled over by Roly. An older man, he was tipped for a great future. His paintings were exciting and eye-catching. Roly was different from anyone she had met before. Roly was a genius. Roly was hers for ever. But Roly had other ideas.

He left college first, protesting everlasting devotion but making earnest speeches about an artist having to be free. She had not seen him since. She had grown up (as she saw it) very quickly, determined never again would she let anyone close enough to hurt her so.

The big dog jumped about with excitement.

'Behave yourself, Ailsa!'

Roly set Kate down on her feet and beamed at her.

'Admiring the boat? Isn't she a beauty? Come inside and have a coffee and we'll tell each other everything!'

They might have only parted yesterday.

Kate was staring at Ailsa.

'Goodness, Roly! Isn't that the pup

you got in your last term at college?'

Roly looked fondly at the dog.

'Yes — and she's a beauty too!'

He helped Kate into the aft cockpit. The paintings on the folded back cabin doors were of vivid colourful outdoor scenes. Down in the tiny cabin Kate gasped. It seemed crowded with ornaments, little lace curtains hung everywhere, there were crochet mats and all the woodwork was brightly painted. There were fittings of gleaming brass; seaside souvenir pots and dishes and 'lace-edged' plates were grouped on the small shelves.

'Great isn't it?' said Roly proudly. 'See — this cupboard door comes down to form a table. Pull this knob and you'll find a folding bed stored under here. This part of the boat has been kept as it always was.'

'And a boatman's whole family lived in here?' said Kate, awed.

'Yes, indeed. I sleep in it now. The rest of the boat has been modernised but I prefer this atmosphere. But we have a little galley through there and all mod. cons.'

He disappeared through a further small door.

Kate sat down on a handy stool. This, too, had been lavishly decorated with roses, daisies and hearts.

Roly reappeared with two mugs of coffee.

'I remember that you don't take sugar,' he said proudly. 'Let's go outside again.'

The sun was warm, the coffee hot. They sat on wooden bench seats and looked at each other with delight. All the carefree days of student life came rushing back.

'Begin!' Roly commanded.

'You remember that I had another year to go at the time that you left. Then I did another year on picture restoring. It's not what I want to do — I want to paint. But — goodness — how does one earn a living as a painter? Commercial art?'

Roly nodded. He understood. It was

every art student's predicament.

'I thought — I can't settle down yet. In any case it isn't easy to get regular work of any kind. So I'm a vagabond. I find painting jobs as I go about. Inn signs, shop fronts, café murals, festival posters. It's surprising what there is if you keep talking to everyone. And I paint the wild flowers for my own satisfaction.'

'And what brought you to the Rose Ann?'

'I did an inn sign in Bridgedale, a few miles off. I like doing inn signs. This was the Saracen's Head.'

'Yes, girl, yes. And?'

'And someone at the pub told me I could see real narrow-boat art work on the canal. So here I am.'

She tilted her head on one side like a hungry blackbird looking at a worm.

'Any work for me, kind sir?'

'Don't mock me, woman! There is, there is! I wouldn't let just anyone do it, either, and I haven't the time myself. In any case, it's not my kind of thing, but with your restoration expertise and delicacy of touch you'll be just the right person. Did you notice the paintings on the barge?'

'Did I? You're joking!'

'Of course I am. The thing is, they need touching up rather badly. It's not a job for any old boat painter and, as I said, not my kind of thing either.'

Kate thought back to Roly's paintings. Huge garish canvases; streaks of this, splotches of that. Splendid stuff but scarcely a preparation for the meticulous work needed on the boat decorations. While her own preference for flower painting had given her a steady hand and a sharp eye for detail.

'What do you say? You can sleep on the boat while you're working. There's plenty of space in the new bit.'

Kate put down her empty mug.

'Roly,' she said, 'it's you who are the angel.'

'Mind you,' said Roly, 'there's no money in it. Just bed and board. And materials, of course.'

The sun went down behind the willows leaving a crimson afterglow on the undersides of far off rain clouds. A passing boat agitated the canal water and little flakes of light tipped the wavelets as they moved to slap against the sides of the Rose Ann. The air began to cool. Kate sighed with satisfaction as she looked around.

'You're on,' she said.

\* \* \*

The cabin was tiny; a bunk, a minute wardrobe. But it managed a small wash-basin and electric light which was presumably battery-powered.

Kate was glad to see there was a key in the door lock. Not that she had the least suspicion of Roly's intentions. But she always battened the door in strange places, as every young woman should. It had become a habit.

She got into bed and pulled the quilt up to her chin, relishing the cool, clean cotton, and wriggled her bare toes as she stretched her legs. A duck quacked loudly outside on the water and a distant owl cried its melancholy call.

Was she really surprised at running into Roly after all this time? Or had she been secretly hoping? She knew his parents' home to be somewhere in the area. Was she pleased or disappointed? She liked him so much but had realised instantly that now he held no magic for her. It had all gone. Indeed, she found it hard to imagine why she had once hungered for his kisses. Roly had been part of student life — and a very nice part too. A niggling doubt had been laid to rest. She belonged only to herself.

Kate woke in the morning to a feeling of extreme well-being. She could smell the dank scent of the canal water but also the appetising aromas of fried bacon and fresh coffee. Quickly she washed, shrugged into sweater and jeans, and padded up the narrow passage to join Roly in the galley.

After breakfast she inspected the

strange landscapes on the cabin doors. Against a background of blue sky and peaked mountains stood a fanciful castle with several conical turrets. On one side it was abutted by a bridge under which water flowed. There was a lake in the background with a small sailing boat and a few clouds in the sky.

Kate studied the panels with interest.

'Naive art, would you say? Very striking; very rich.'

'This is typical of the best narrow boat work.'

'I shall have to get books. Research a bit before I dare touch it.'

'No problem. I've already done that. Just in case I had to have a go at it myself. Luckily I still have one old book from the local library on board. It explains the techniques as far as they are known.'

'Great. Then I'll need to go into town for materials.'

'That's easy. There's a bus once a day that passes the other end of the lane. I'll give you some money.'

'You'll have to do that. Hand-to-mouth is the way I live now.'

Roly laughed.

'What's new about that? Didn't we always — as students?'

Fortunately the weather stayed dry. For the next week Kate worked blissfully to bring back the original clear colours to the door panels. She was absorbed in the work. She knew she was lucky. For the moment she had food, shelter, congenial company and a job that she was good at and which was tremendously worth doing.

One evening they wandered along the towpath to the Bargeman's Rest. It was warm enough to sit outside the pub with their drinks.

Kate looked critically at the inn sign which showed an old-time narrowboat, apparently loaded with coal, and decided to offer her services as sign painter as soon as she'd finished this job for Roly.

On the way back to the boat Roly suddenly stopped.

'Look at me, Kate!'

His arms went round her and he kissed her on the lips.

'Don't, Roly!'

She struggled and pushed but he held on and kissed her again.

Exasperated, Kate kicked him hard on the shins.

He yelped, let her go, and rubbed his leg.

'What did you do that for?'

He sounded aggrieved.

'You don't really want to kiss me. It's just an old habit. I might take you seriously and move in on you and you wouldn't like that. We're loners, you and I. You know that.'

'Speak for yourself! Anyway, Kate — you're a dish and a bloke's got to try. It's my macho self-image!' explained Roly.

She could just see the grin above his beard in the dusk.

'I enjoyed it,' he said.

Ailsa stood on the roof of the barge keeping guard. There was no need to keep her tied up; she was a most obedient dog. But now, with a great leap, she was down and frolicking around them.

'Good girl, Ailsa,' said Roly. '*You* love me, don't you?'

* * *

The sun was very hot. So hot that the tendrils of red-gold hair which curled prettily over the white nape of her neck were sticky with sweat. She was very, very carefully working on the roses. She was happy.

A shadow fell across the side of the boat.

'What the devil do you think you are doing?' demanded a man's voice harshly.

Kate's hand slipped and she swore.

'How dare you?' she snapped. 'Can't you see this is delicate work?'

She removed her hand carefully,

blew gently on the design and turned round.

'I said: 'What are you doing?' he repeated, blue eyes dark and hard.

'I should have thought any fool could see that I'm retouching this design,' retorted Kate. 'And if you knew anything at all about it you wouldn't creep up behind and shout at me. It's important — and not at all easy — to get it exactly right.'

'And what do *you* know about it?'

Kate felt a flush of rage staining her cheeks.

'Roses and castles. Traditional narrow boat decoration. No-one knows quite how it started. Some say the boatmen were gypsies who took to the water and brought with them their cart painting techniques.'

The stranger raised his eyebrows. Kate continued, carried away by her enthusiasm:

'Others say that when the railways came and wages on the canals were cut, men brought their wives and families to live on the boats and painted them up to make them homey. They saw great houses from the water and put them into their designs. Mind you, I have a theory of my own . . .'

'Yes,' he said impatiently, 'that's the history side of it. But what do you know of the technique?'

'I am an artist,' replied Kate coldly. 'And also a qualified picture restorer. And the owner has engaged me to restore these.'

'The *owner*?' he queried.

Kate looked at him scornfully.

'Oh, do go away,' she begged. 'I was getting on so well before you came along.'

At that moment she heard an ecstatic 'woof' and Alisa pranced across the quay and hurled herself lovingly at the man standing there.

'Down, dog!' he commanded, pushing her in the chest with both hands, but not before his face had been anointed with several slurping salutes.

Roly followed. He had been up to

the village for stores. Now he slung his back-pack down on to the stones and strode forwards.

'Giles! I wasn't expecting you!'

'So I see,' said the other man dryly. 'Introduce me to your friend.'

Roly looked a little embarrassed.

'This is Kate Trevine. She was at art college with me. (Do get up, Kate!) I've engaged her to do the tricky part of the painting. It's all right. I'm not *paying* her anything. Just bed and board.'

'I *see*. Just bed and board.'

Kate went a fiery red. She scrambled to her feet, furiously angry. The implication of the last remark was obvious.

She looked at Roly accusingly.

'Does this mean you are not the owner? I thought she was your boat.'

'So she is,' retorted Roly, 'because I'm the captain. I never said I was the owner.'

But he seemed a bit abashed.

'Good heavens, girl, where did you

think I'd get the kind of money that would buy a converted narrow-boat? Giles hired me for the summer. I live on board and he pays me a salary to have her ready for him any time. Where else could I keep Alisa with me. Oh — Kate! This is Giles Harcourt.'

Kate was wiping her hands on a piece of rag soaked in white spirits. Her heart had sunk into her trainers. Was this the end of it? She had hoped that Roly and she could turn the boat so that she could complete the renovation with the other side.

Would this Giles Harcourt want her to continue? He seemed to think she'd been damaging his property.

Now that her temper had cooled a little she was able to take in the appearance of the newcomer. It was depressing. His hair was smartly cut; he was clean shaven. Crisp light grey suit; white shirt and a blue tie to match his eyes. Shoes of pale grey suede. Everything discreetly of the best.

And everything consequently shouting: 'I am rich!'

He bent down and subjected her work to a minute inspection. At once Kate felt ruffled again.

'Yes,' he said. 'I do apologise. I can see you know what you are doing. I'm sorry I interrupted.'

He turned to Roly.

'How's it going? I'm bringing some business friends along for a trip at the end of the week. Will she be ready?'

'The engine's running to perfection,' said Roly enthusiastically. 'Will you be fetching the stores or do you want me to get them in?'

'I'll bring them. Oh — by the way — Margy is coming to help you out as usual. She'll do the food and the domestic bit. Let me know if there's anything else you need.'

The two men disappeared into the boat.

'Well!' said Kate, scratching Ailsa behind one ear. 'I suppose that means

I'm allowed to finish the job. They might have said!'

But she felt edgy and her hand shook as she began carefully to clean her brushes. The day was spoiled.

# 2

Giles Harcourt had gone. Peace settled over the Rose Ann once more. Gnats danced in clouds over the water; a blackbird fluted melodiously from the top of an alder tree.

Kate warmed her hands on a mug of after supper coffee and gazed broodingly across the canal.

'Do you like that man?' she asked abruptly.

'Who — Giles? Yes, I do. I needed a job when he met me in a local pub. He's all right. Lets me do everything my way so long as the boat's ready when he wants it.'

'Rich business men,' said Kate with loathing. 'I suppose it's just an ego-trip for him. Having something old and beautiful that other people can't afford.'

Roly looked at her thoughtfully.

'It's not quite like that but — do you think that she's beautiful? I do.'

'Yes. And I'm honoured to be able to help keep her that way.'

Later, as she lay in her bunk listening to the night sounds, she wondered what she would find to do next. This was the perfect job in so many ways but she needed to earn. Meanwhile she would enjoy finishing the job in hand.

Roly said it would not be possible to turn the boat. It was too long and the canal too narrow. But the opposite bank, though not paved, had a firm surface and so he manoeuvred the Rose Ann across.

Kate settled down to refurbish the decorations on the other side. She worked happily away bringing back the brightness to the gilded frame edging; the red and pink and blue to the petals of the formal roses. She forgot about Giles Harcourt and the fact that this job was nearly over in the pleasure of practising her craft.

It was not quick and easy to do,

for other boats went by and then the Rose Ann dipped and swayed and her mooring ropes creaked. Kate had to squat back on her heels and wait for the motion to cease.

It took three more days of concentrated effort but at last it was completed to her satisfaction. They got the boat back to her original moorings and Roly examined and complimented her on her work.

'You've done a beautiful job, Kate. What luck that you turned up.'

'Yes,' said Kate, looking critically at a fairy-tale castle which gleamed against an eggshell blue sky. 'And it's been great fun, Roly, but now I must be on my way. I've got my bread and butter to earn.'

'I suppose you must go. But don't let us lose touch again.'

'Perhaps I'll come back this way. Are you usually here?'

'I go where the boss tells me but we don't stay out for more than a few days as a rule. If you ring the Bargeman's

Rest they know my movements.'

'Right. I'll get my stuff together.'

She stood on tiptoes and gave him a hug and a kiss for old times' sake, then disappeared into the boat.

Giles Harcourt emerged from the lane and came across the flagstones. He looked harassed. Roly, used to Giles' habit of suddenly appearing waved a hand towards the Rose Ann.

'Done a good job, has Kate. You'll be pleased.' But Giles showed no interest.

'Look Roly, you know I've got guests coming tomorrow? But Margy's let me down. She's gone off to town on one of her flings.'

'Why now?' Roly was upset. 'I must have a side-kick. Can't steer the ship, run the engine, work the locks *and* get the meals.'

'It's a damned nuisance,' said Giles gloomily. 'These aren't the sort of people I can ask to muck in. I've promised them a couple of days lazing around.'

It was then that Kate dropped her kit over the side onto the quay and jumped down after it.

Giles swung round and stared at her.

'That's it! What about you?'

'What about me?' echoed Kate, looking at him blankly.

'Margy, who usually devils for Roly, has gone off for the weekend and we're taking the Rose Ann out tomorrow. You could fill in. How about it?'

Kate stared at him with an expression of incredulity.

'Are you asking me — so nicely — to help you out of a spot?'

'That's it.'

'You can get lost,' she said succinctly. 'I don't work for people with no manners.'

'I'll pay you, of course,' he said indifferently.

'Well, of course!' Kate's green eyes sparked fire. 'Your type think they can buy anything. But I'm not for sale!'

She bent and hoisted her back-pack

on to her shoulders.

'Goodbye, Roly. I've enjoyed it all a lot.'

Roly was lounging in a relaxed manner with his hands in his pockets and he looked amused. He rather liked to see Kate when her temper was rising.

Giles was looking at her properly for the first time. What he saw was a sturdy young woman with springing red curls and long green eyes on whose unusually creamy cheekbones and the bridge of a small, resolute nose the sun had brought out a flock of honey coloured freckles. She did not appear to be in the least interested in the job he was offering.

But he needed help and he needed it quickly. He was much too astute to switch to pleading politeness.

'I see,' he said coldly. 'You are afraid of real work, are you?'

Kate spun round.

'What do you mean? I work hard!'

'That's not *work*.'

26

He laughed dismissively. 'I don't suppose you can lift anything heavier than a paint brush.'

'Of course I can,' snapped Kate. 'I'm as competent as anyone.'

'Oh yes? So why won't you take up my offer? It's only for a weekend. You can earn good money and prove your point.'

'I'm an artist, not a dogsbody!'

Giles looked scornful. Kate glared at him. Suddenly she wrenched off her pack and dumped it back on the quay.

'Right!' she said. 'Just for this trip.'

Over the top of her head as she turned away Giles gave the merest flicker of a wink. Roly grinned.

★ ★ ★

The Rose Ann had been scoured and polished until everything shone. Bunks had been made up and fresh towels laid out, stores checked and Roly consulted about the kind of meals Giles Harcourt

27

expected for his guests. The food and drink was all of the highest quality and the little galley fitted with every modern convenience.

Kate saw no reason why she should not be able to manage admirably.

The car that pulled up almost at the water's edge late on Friday evening was low and sporty with an open top. It was finished in a dull gold which glittered in the rays of the setting sun.

Giles Harcourt, dressed in casual gear, got out of the driving seat and opened the doors for his guests.

The young woman who eased herself fluidly from the front seat had that kind of casual chic that always made Kate feel dowdy. She wore a shocking pink T-shirt with matching sneakers and her slacks were of a particular linen-look tan which suggested Brittany rather than Britain. Her hair was dark and sleek and smooth and caught at the back with a matching pink ribbon. Kate, who was wearing an over-size blue shirt with the sleeves rolled up, felt like the odd-job man.

The other two guests were elderly and plump and American. They looked amiable and interested. The man was balding and the woman an improbable blonde.

Giles said: 'Here are Kate and Roly who will be looking after us this weekend. Rod and Dulcie Merton from the States and Rowenda Lucas.'

The Americans shook hands and repeated names. Rowenda's glance slid over Kate but fastened appreciatively on Roly. Kate steeled herself. She felt this was going to be a very, very trying weekend.

'I'll show you to your cabins,' she invited.

Presently the party was sitting on canvas chairs in the forward cockpit, the ladies with gin-and-tonic and the gentlemen with Scotch. Kate could have done with a drink herself but none was offered so she went back to join Roly and Ailsa.

Roly had taken the car and stowed it

in a stone shed by the quayside. Now he was polishing the engine. Kate busied herself arranging a big bunch of wild flowers, cow-parsley, pink campion, a few bluebells and yellow buttercups, in a green tin water-can which had been splendidly decorated with white daisies and pink roses and edged with red and gold lines.

The sun was almost down and the air had begun to chill.

Giles put his head out of the cabin door. 'We're all off to bed. Early start tomorrow,' he said.

★ ★ ★

Breakfast over, Roly started the engine, which chuntered softly. Kate slipped the mooring lines over the bollards and jumped on board. The boat moved away from the quay.

At first it was idyllic. She watched Roly work the enormous rudder with Ailsa sitting by his side. Buildings soon slipped away. The banks were wooded and sunshine dappled through leaves. Drifts of bluebells lay beneath and a cuckoo called loudly and quite close.

Kate served lunch in the small saloon. Colourful and assorted salads mixed in big wooden bowls; French sticks warm from the oven; several cheeses; chocolate mousse with whipped cream. Giles served his guests sparkling white wine. Afterwards there was coffee with small sugar-coated biscuits.

The engine had settled down to a pleasant 'chug chug' and the banks went past very slowly, for the speed limit was strict. Kate and Roly ate sandwiches in the aft cockpit and drank beer out of cans as the boat pottered along the canal.

They went under a hump-backed bridge, the shadow making them suddenly cold, and out into sunny meadows where cows grazed.

Presently Kate went back to clear away and wash up.

She had just stowed the last dish when a shout from Roly brought her out again. The Rose Ann had stopped. There was a wooden barrier across the canal.

'Out you get, my girl,' said Roly. 'This is where you learn a new trick. It's called 'working a lock.'

# 3

'But I don't know how!'

'You take this,' Roly handed her a windlass, which looked to Kate a cross between a large square-ended spanner and a car cranking handle, 'and you fix it onto the spindle on that metal post and it turns the cog-wheels that raise the paddle.'

'What paddle?' asked Kate, quite confused.

'The paddle that covers a hole down there in the water at the bottom of the gate. Drawing the paddle lets the water into the lock and when it's level with us you can open the gate and we go in. *Then* you draw the paddle at the other end, the water goes down, and you can open the gate at that end and out we go — several feet lower.'

'Oh! Can I do all that by myself?' asked Kate doubtfully.

'Of course you can. No sweat. Small boys do it.'

'I dare say they know what they are doing,' said Kate caustically, 'which I do not. Okay, I'll have a go.'

She scrambled on shore and peered over the gate and down at the water which seemed a long way away. Then she fixed the windlass and tried to turn the mechanism. Either it was stiff or she was clumsy because nothing seemed to happen. She pushed harder.

'Some small boy,' she muttered.

A voice said in her ear.

'Excuse me. I think there may be a safety catch on.'

A hand came round.

'Now try.'

She pushed the windlass again and it moved, creaking the while. Giles was standing close behind her.

'That's the way,' he said encouragingly, 'but you need a little more weight on it.'

His arms went round each side of her, his hands gripped just above hers and they turned together. Kate could hear the water rushing into the lock. It seemed a long time before Giles stepped back.

Kate looked over the gate. The water was now on a level with that on which the boat floated.

'You see the wooden beam?' said Giles. 'You lean on that and, now that the water is level, the gate will open. You won't find it hard. Take it slowly.'

It was true. Kate stood with her back against the beam and pushed. Gradually, as it moved round, the big gate opened. Roly gently eased the Rose Ann into the lock. The visitors were all out watching.

Once the boat had safely moved forwards Kate closed the top gate and lowered the paddle. Then she was directed to the other end, where she did it all over again. This time the raised paddle let the water out and the Rose Ann sank in a stately manner, down between dripping black walls.

Ailsa continued to sit by Roly and seemed quite unconcerned; she had done it many times before.

When the Rose Ann emerged from her slippery-sided cell Kate closed the second gate and paddle before they got back on board.

Kate felt a great sense of achievement. 'That was fun,' she said.

'Well done,' said Giles with a smile.

Kate felt uncomfortably breathless. Was this the result of the effort needed in 'working the lock' or of the close proximity of a man who, she assured herself, she did not like at all?

The rest of the day the Rose Ann proceeded gently between flat fields. Yellow water iris and golden marsh-marigolds brightened the banks. Swallows flashed and dipped to the water after insects. A pair of white-faced coot scuttled along the canal edge.

Kate made a tray of tea. In the saloon Giles was sitting at the table next to the sleek Rowenda. There were papers spread before them and their heads were close together. As Kate came in she heard Rowenda laugh. Giles raised his head, tossing back an unruly lock of hair.

'Thanks, Kate,' he said, taking two mugs and setting one before his companion.

'Thanks Kate,' echoed Rowenda.

But both sounded preoccupied and the salutation seemed merely routine. Why not? But Kate felt obscurely put down as she went on her way to the forward cockpit where the American couple were watching the scene go by.

'Thanks, honey.' Dulcie Merton pushed her wide straw hat on to the back of her head and smiled warmly at Kate.

'You sure are a busy lady.'

'Gee, yes,' said Rod. 'She spoils us rotten. Isn't all this the greatest?' He waved a pudgy hand at the passing view. 'It's really truly England just as we've always imagined.'

'Our folks came from these parts way back,' confided Dulcie.

The natural friendless of the Americans made Kate feel a lot better.

The Rose Ann pulled in for the night where a path led away from the canal across a field.

'There's a pub up there,' said Roly. 'We're all going later on. The Blue Anchor. A real old one with oak settles and board floors and the landlady's a character. The Yanks will love it.'

Kate served the evening meal.

A casserole fragrant with herbs, hot granary bread, fresh fruit salad and the cheese board. As she cleared away the dishes Giles said: 'Coming to the pub, Kate? We're all going.'

'Yes, do come, honey,' cried Dulcie, 'it'll be such fun!'

Kate addressed her reply to Dulcie Merton.

'It does sound nice but I'm really a bit tired. I think I'd better have an early night.'

She did not look at Giles.

'That's a shame,' said Rod, heavily. 'We'll miss you, kid. That boss of yours works you too hard!' He looked with reproof at Giles. 'But you go and have a nice rest if that's what you'd like.'

Going rather pink and smiling at the Americans, Kate fled into the galley. She had caught a sardonic look from Giles. It was a shame. She'd really have liked to be one of the party but she felt too prickly to be sociable.

And she was tired. Despite her brave words to Giles her bones ached. It was a long time since she had been through so much hard physical labour.

Kate made sure that everything was spotless before she went to bed. There was no-one there to see how she slammed things about to placate the seething indignation inside. Why? She had chosen to stay behind.

She was drowsing in her bunk when the party came home. She heard laughter and voices. Roly adjuring Dulcie not to fall in. Squeaks and giggles from the lady and a deep rumbling laugh from Rod. Then calls of 'goodnight' and an exchange between Giles and Rowenda which ended in soft words which tailed away.

★ ★ ★

Church bells sounded across the meadows as they made their way back up the canal. They passed another narrow boat and so found the lock already set for their entry. This time Giles took the tiller and Roly joined Kate in working the lock, so there was nothing to worry her. She watched the water rise and the boat with it until the top gate swung easily when she leaned on the beam.

It was late afternoon and they were back in the dappled light and shade of the woods. Kate felt able to leave the boat and walk along the tow path. After a time Giles jumped ashore and walked with her. She wished he would not. She wanted to be alone with her own thoughts. Listening to the wood noises and the soft 'chug' of the engine.

'This is very pleasant,' said Giles. 'You did a good job on the paintings, Kate.'

'Thank you.'

She couldn't help feeling pleased.

'You said you had a theory of your own about the roses and castles motif. What is that?'

'Well,' said Kate, 'it's just a story I made up. Some of the castles have conical turrets and look rather like the illustrations in a French fairy tale book I had as a child.'

'Some of the castles are very Eastern looking,' objected Giles. 'And some roses — Damask roses — are said to have been brought here by the Crusaders.'

'Real roses?'

'Yes — real roses,' said Giles, with an amused look down.

'The castles I am thinking of remind me of the Chateaux of the Loire. And they none of them look at all like great English country houses.'

'So what is your story?'

'I like to think that there was once an artist whose patron was a French Duc. But the revolution came and his aristocratic family fell into trouble. The artist had to flee. He came to England and became an itinerant painter working along the canals. Because his lord's escutcheon bore roses that was what he painted — and because he was homesick he conjured up the castle from which he came.'

'Oh,' said Giles. 'They don't look at all like English country houses? I wouldn't be too sure about that. But it's a pretty story.'

'Thank you,' said Kate, rather stiffly. She wondered why she had laid herself open to being mocked. The trouble was that the man had a lot of charm when he chose to use it.

'Now don't ruffle up,' he said, 'at least your idea is original. I can see its appeal — you're an itinerant painter yourself, after all!'

'We'd better get back to the boat,' said Kate, quickening her pace, 'it must be time for serving tea.'

Giles kept up with her easily.

'Just let me thank you, Kate. You've really done a great job of support for me. We couldn't have managed without you.'

'I think you could — if you'd made a bit of an effort yourself. I think it's damned cheek telling *me* I never do any real work.'

'Like you — I consider my work is very real.'

'Huh!' said Kate, and tossed her head.

Giles tried hard not to laugh; she looked so like an indignant child.

It was dusk when they docked. Roly fetched the golden car from the stone shed where it had been waiting. Rowenda shook hands with Kate and thanked her for a great trip. So did Dulcie Merton. But when Kate withdrew her hand from Rod's hearty grip she was astonished and mortified to find in it several folded bank notes. She turned bright red.

'But . . . but . . . '

Rod beamed at her in a fatherly manner and patted her shoulder.

'Think nothing of it. You earned every cent! It was the trip of a lifetime!'

Kate gazed at him in consternation. She couldn't push back the gratuity to this kind and friendly man. He wasn't to know that she had never been tipped before in her life and it made her feel most peculiar.

'I hope we meet again, honey,' said Dulcie kindly.

'Sure do,' confirmed Rod.

Rowenda was saying 'goodbye' to Roly and patting Ailsa on the head.

Giles said: 'Thanks, Kate.' He held out his hand. 'We will meet again. I know it.'

His hand was warm and firm and held hers for rather longer than seemed necessary. She drew hers away.

'I don't think so,' she said, 'but it has

been a very interesting experience.'

His eyes crinkled at the corners when he smiled.

'Is that all? Interesting? Oh dear!'

She turned away. He could be quite nice when he chose. But he'd certainly tricked her into short-term servitude when he played on her temper to get her working on his boat.

She stood with Roly to watch the guests depart. It was Rowenda who got into the driving seat, set the gaudy vehicle in gear and drove away up the lane.

'Isn't that Giles' car, then?'

'I should think not!' exclaimed Roly, shocked. 'What sort of a wimp do you think he is?'

No — Giles Harcourt was not a wimp. He might be a slick bossy business man, well equipped with the necessary charm, but he was not a wimp.

Roly and Kate went for a last drink at the Bargeman's Arms. Kate planned to leave the Rose Ann in the morning. She was still brooding over Rod's generous hand-out.

'Did Giles' guests tip Margy?' she enquired.

Roly hooted.

'If they did she never told me but I'm damned sure she'd have pocketed it and been delighted.'

'In that case I'll not fuss. It's just something I'm not used to.'

She gazed thoughtfully up at old Bill's tatty sign.

'How about hiring me to do you a new sign?' she asked.

The landlord looked horrified.

'What would I want that for? Been the same sign for years and that's the way I like it.'

'It could do with brightening up,' urged Kate.

'Nay, lass. That it could not. My customers would all be frightened away.'

'Oh well,' Kate sighed, and took a refreshing swig of her shandy. 'I need another job.'

'Tell you what — you go to the White Swan. Vera's sign was knocked down in a storm a few weeks ago, I hear tell, happen she'd be right glad to see you.'

'Thanks Bill. I'll do that.'

She said 'goodbye' to Roly in the morning, shouldered her pack and set off. It was strange leaving the Rose Ann. Almost like leaving home again.

# 4

'So Bill sent you, did he? I've heard about you. Did a good job for the Saracen's Head, so they say.'

Vera leaned plump arms on the bar and inspected Kate. The room was very clean with a mixed scent of soap and polish and beer. The flagstones of the floor were still damp from a recent scrubbing and the ceiling beams were low and hung with bright horse brasses. You could see the adze marks on the old wood.

The landlady was evidently pleased with what she saw for she smiled and said: 'Dump your pack down, lass, and say what you fancy.'

Soon Kate was perched on a wooden bar stool sipping her usual shandy.

Vera Dan was a widow who ran the pub on her own.

'I'll be right glad of your company

for a while, lass. I can give you a bed and I'm well known round here for good home baking. You do right by me and I'll do right by you.'

★ ★ ★

Kate missed the Rose Ann and the feeling of floating at night. She missed the sound of the water birds. The White Swan was some way from the canal.

But it was a pleasant life. She worked in the old dairy which was very clean and had a big window with a view over farm land to the edge of the moors. Sometimes it rained and the view was obscured. But when it was fine she could work with the door open. It faced away from the back of the pub and was quite secluded.

Directly opposite the open door grew a large May tree which was covered with fragrant white blossom. Wild flowers grew on the edge of the meadow.

Sometimes, to make a change as

she waited for the shiny waterproof paint on the sign to dry, Kate drew pencil sketches: field poppies and cornflowers displayed amongst green wheat. Then she lovingly coloured them with watercolour. She enjoyed doing this best of all.

In the evenings Vera shared with her splendid home-baked meals and gossip about her early life.

Afterwards in the bar Kate was very popular with the regulars, slow speaking farmworkers who took a very good view of having a young and attractive red-headed lass to brighten up their drinking hours.

But, for the first time since she had left home to earn her way on the road, Kate was restless. She often found her thoughts returning to the Rose Ann. It must, she decided, be due to meeting Roly again. It had stirred up memories of the free and easy days with all her student friends at art college. Up till now she had relished the vagrant life she had been leading. She had never felt lonely, always looking forward to the next adventure. Pleased that she was managing to live without being incarcerated in a stuffy office; without having to commute every day by train or bus or car to toil in some big city.

'Drat the man!' she thought. 'Why did I have to bump into him?'

But she wouldn't have wanted to miss the Rose Ann, would she? Did she think of Giles at all? She pushed him out of her mind.

She took a lot of trouble with the swan. She carried a small bird book with her which she studied to get the details right.

It was a mute swan, she decided: very large, very white, with bright, dark eyes and an orange bill with a black knob underneath. The neck snaked gracefully up, the great wings were slightly raised, the beak a little open as though the bird was hissing. It was a cob, a king swan, and on the proud head Kate placed a coronet of gold.

She ate her sandwiches in the bar at lunch time where it was cool and pleasant. There was another small room, called the saloon bar, through an arch, with its own bit of counter. None of the locals drank there.

A car pulled up and a door clicked. After a moment a small hand bell sounded. One of the local men peered through the arch. He turned to Vera: 'There's strangers in there!' he said with a deep disgust. Kate no longer counted as a stranger.

Vera went along to serve.

That section of the counter ran at an angle to the rest so that drinkers at the long bar could see the customers at the other.

There were two men. Both wore business suits and white shirts with collar and tie. They did not look like tourists. Travelling salesmen, perhaps, on their way to town or one of the big farms.

Yet they seemed to be interested in local historic buildings, for one asked:

'Court Castle? Is that nearby?'

'Not so far,' said Vera, pulling a pint of the best and pushing it over.

The taller man, who had wide shoulders, sipped his beer and asked: 'National Trust, would it be?'

'No indeed. A private house.'

'Ah, well. No use to us then.'

He glanced down at his friend who was thinner and shorter and drinking cider. The friend looked pensively down into his drink.

'That's right,' he said.

'Not interested in roses then? said Vera. 'Best in the country, they have.'

'Roses?' said the taller man. 'No, indeed. We are looking at ruins and such like.'

'There's Brindale Fort on the edge of the moor.'

'How would we get there?'

'Back up the main road for a couple of miles and you'll see it signposted. Nowt but crumbling walls but if you like that sort of thing . . . ' They left after one drink, thanking Vera politely.

The pub regulars settled back with a sigh of relief. High season, you expected all sorts to find their way to the White Swan but not so many got here in the middle of a working day in May. Unsettled the day.

The afternoon was hot. Too hot for work. Kate curled down on a rug under the May tree, breathed the sweet scent of the flowers and watched little white clouds drift across the smooth blue sky. Her eyelids felt heavy. She drowsed and slept.

She woke with a start, thinking she was back on the Rose Ann and for a moment an unexpected feeling of bitter disappointment swept over her. She gave herself a shake. This was a good job. She was lucky. She went back to her swan.

Among the rushes on the bank she placed yellow iris, and, working with tiny delicate strokes, scattered small yellow water lilies on the river. She loved painting flowers.

May had turned to June by the

time the sign was finished to her satisfaction. Vera came and approved it, hands on hips and a considering expression. Then she smiled broadly.

'It's a peach. Better than any in the district, I'll be bound. Worth every penny and more.'

She turned to Kate.

'Tell you what. We'll have a regular ceremony for the hanging. The Royal Academy won't see anything like it.'

They had it one hot sunny lunchtime with free beer all round and sausages on sticks. The sign swung there with all its colours glowing and fresh and a cheer went up.

Everyone was laughing and congratulating Kate. The air smelled of the fresh cut grass as it was crushed under their feet. She felt useful and cherished and then suddenly it was all over. She was alone again with Vera.

'A nice cup of tea is what we both need,' said Vera, and they went back into the pub.

Kate drank the tea and felt better.

'Oh well,' she said, 'it's been great staying here, Vera. But now I must be on my way. I have to look for another job. You don't know of one, I suppose?'

'By the time my swan has been talked about all round the county every pub in the district will be after you! Yes — I have heard of someone who has work for you. But I think it is something to do with pictures, not inn signs. Up at Court Castle.'

'Court Castle? Now where have I heard that name before? I remember! There were some men in the saloon one day asking for it.'

'It isn't all that far away. If you go down to the canal you can walk along the tow path for two or three miles. You can see it from there. It's a grand sight.'

Kate thought that she would like to get back to the canal. Walking beside water would be pleasant. She needn't hurry.

'No need to go until tomorrow,' said Vera. 'I'll be sorry to lose you, to tell the truth. It's been nice to have another woman around.'

In the morning Kate packed up her things and gave Vera a hug.

'Who will I ask for?'

'Mrs Harcourt — Harcourt Castle is rightly the name of the house.'

'Oh!'

She might have expected that Giles Harcourt would live in a mansion. Could she bear to work for his wife and probably have to meet him every day? He was conceited and overbearing and she didn't like him at all. She was sure his wife would be cold and elegant and Kate would find herself in the servants quarters being patronised by the family and their guests.

She said cautiously: 'Are they all right? As people, I mean? I've never worked for a private family before.'

Vera laughed.

'The Harcourts? Been here for generations. Greatly respected in the district. You'll be all right, child. Don't you worry about that.'

There were wild roses with gold hearts and pale pink heart-shaped petals; there were great clusters of creamy blossom on the elder. A moorhen scuttled along the canal bank. Everything was peaceful.

Kate walked slowly. There was no hurry and she had a lot to think about. One half of her mind rejected the idea of working for the Harcourts; the other realised that she was not in a position to refuse. She was, after all, a freelance. It was not reasonable to reject a job unless it was one she felt unqualified to undertake. Furthermore she had been long enough in the area to appreciate how fast and efficient was the bush telegraph.

Supposing she didn't go to Court Castle? (What a pretentious name for a house.) Everyone at the White Swan knew that was where Kate was heading. If she was discourteous and disobliging to a respected local family she wouldn't be welcome anywhere else. Who, round here, would want to employ her knowing that she'd given Giles' family the brush-off? She would have to move out of the district.

Somehow she didn't want to.

She sat down by the side of the canal and ate her sandwiches. A canal boat passed by, brightly painted but not (in Kate's opinion) as pretty as the Rose Ann. The holiday makers on board smiled and waved and called out a cheerful 'good morning'. The canal waters sloshed against the side of the cut and the slow 'chug chug' of the engine made Kate feel quite nostalgic.

'Never mind,' she told herself, 'one day when I'm rich I'll have a holiday on a narrow-boat too.'

It was a strange life she led, making friends and leaving them. But it meant she had time to do her own thing and her sketchbook was filling up with portraits of wild flowers and with notes of the locations and dates. There was something about flowers, with their intricate structure and fragile fleeting life; with their infinite variety of shapes and colours and scents; the way they marked the passage of the seasons. They had a special place in her heart and she could go on for ever trying to capture their essence on paper. Unfortunately she had not yet thought of a way to harness her obsession to the business of making a living. Perhaps one day she would do a book — but meanwhile one must eat.

After lunch Kate walked on. There were no locks this way, the land lay flat at the foot of a slope. Presently the path was blocked by a stone-edged inlet, a loading bay, just long enough to take one narrow boat. The towpath stopped and started again on the other side of the small bay and a footpath led round the edge and away up the hill. And there, at the top of a long slope thick with the gold of buttercups where a white goat grazed, stood a huge stone house.

As Kate made her way up towards it she stared, for, as what had appeared in the distance as a grey mass became clearer, she could see that battlements topped the facade and at each end of the roof rose a slim, pointed turret.

So this was Court Castle. It was grand indeed.

Kate toiled up the hill amongst the buttercups, bees buzzing in the warm air, and sweat beginning to make the red-gold curls stick to her forehead. She began to wonder what she'd let herself in for. The building was frighteningly large and imposing.

In front of the house the ground fell away in terraces built of stone slabs and on each side of the stepped path cascaded sweet-smelling, small-blossomed roses of pink and cream and yellow. Nervous as she felt, Kate was enraptured by the sight as she pushed open the small iron gate and advanced steadily upwards.

Since she'd come so far she must at

least look at the proffered job. Anyway, she had probably been seen from the house and she couldn't run away. And after all, if the set-up was too starchy and upper-crust to be borne she could always say it wasn't her kind of thing. It was hardly likely to be another inn sign!

She felt better after that thought.

The door was massive, dark wood bound with iron. No electric bell, just an old-fashioned chain. Kate pulled, and a rather melodious booming sounded inside the building.

As Kate waited she imagined the imposing form of a well-trained butler moving down the passage towards her. She braced herself.

The door opened. A small elderly figure stood there, one hand trying unsuccessfully to push some wisps of soft grey hair back into the bun from which they had escaped, the other behind her back fumbling with the ties of a print cotton apron. Kate was glad not to meet the stately butler of her imaginings. This must be the housekeeper.

'Oh dear,' said the little woman guiltily, 'you've caught me in *such* a muddle. You must be Kate Trevine. I'm Mary Harcourt.'

# 5

Kate stepped into a wide, cool hall from which a grand staircase led upwards. Mary Harcourt had pink cheeks and laughter lines around faded blue eyes. Her hand was small but surprisingly strong. She smiled ruefully at Kate and, oddly, turned her back.

'Help me undo this knot, there's a good girl. I was just rinsing the dishes and you know what water does to tapes. Thank you. That's better.'

She whipped off her pinny and was revealed in a blue cotton dress.

'Come into the drawing-room.'

She led Kate through a door into a comfortable-looking room with faded cretonne covers on squashy furniture, matching curtains caught back by tarnished gold cords from tall French windows. White roses drooped from a pink china bowl set on a polished wood table, scattering petals and filling the room with a heavy perfume.

'Do sit down. Would you like some coffee? No — I know just the thing — iced lemonade.'

'Yes, *please*,' said Kate, smiling back.

While her hostess went to fetch the drink Kate looked round. It was a homey room despite its faded grandeur. A fat white cat, who looked very old, opened slits of eyes and glinted at Kate, then sank back into sleep. There were silver ornaments on the marble mantelpiece, duplicated by their reflections in the huge overmantel mirror. Some rather dark landscapes, Victorian in feel, hung on the walls.

Mary Harcourt came back with a tray on which were two tall glasses, the outsides misting in the warm air. Ice clinked invitingly against the side as she handed a glass to Kate.

'Thank you very much, Mrs Harcourt,' said Kate, sipping the cold liquid gratefully. 'I'm not quite sure what it is you hope I can do for you?'

'My son Giles says you are an artist — a good one.'

'That's kind of him,' said Kate, somewhat astonished, 'but I don't know how he knows.'

'You did a splendid job on the Rose Ann and everyone has heard of your inn signs. Of course, this isn't at all the same thing but I hope — I've always wanted to have it done, you see, but one is so busy and time passes so fast . . .'

'But what is it you have in mind?' asked Kate, now thoroughly intrigued. She was beginning to hope it was something she could do for the atmosphere of the house was very enticing and she had taken an instant liking to Mary Harcourt.

'It's a picture I would like to have copied.' Kate glanced at the walls. 'No, no. Nothing like that. This is a portrait. Come and see.'

Kate put down her empty glass and rose to follow the older woman out of the room. They went up the stairs which were wide and shallow and carpeted with a faded tapestry design. The stairs turned at a half-landing and here they stopped.

On the wall directly opposite was an almost life-sized painting in an elaborate gold frame. Kate gazed up, entranced. The young woman in the picture had fair hair bobbed in the fashion of the Twenties, bound with a slim band of green ribbon. The figure was seated, dressed in sea-green gauze, with a short single row of pearls round her neck. Across the hands which rested in her lap, slim fingers curled upwards shell-like, lay a long-stemmed rose with a few green leaves and one fully open many-petalled deep pink flower.

'My husband's mother,' said Mary Harcourt. 'Isn't she lovely? His brother's family live in Australia and they'd so like to have the picture. But of course that's not possible, it belongs here. And then Giles thought — and why did I never think of it myself? — that the thing to do would be to have it copied, now that there is a bit more money. What do you think . . . ' she turned eagerly towards Kate. 'Is it something you could do for me?'

Kate was looking up at the picture. Of course she'd done a lot of copying at art college but this would be a real challenge.

The painting was superb. The texture of the skin palpably soft; the swathes of gaze rendered precisely. She wanted to do it very much indeed but doubted that she was good enough.

The painting was in oils, not her favourite medium. It was very large. Mary Harcourt was watching her hopefully.

'When you say a copy do you mean an exact copy? The same medium and the same size?'

'Oh, no, no. It's got to go to Australia, remember. That would be daunting, wouldn't it?'

'I could do it in water-colour,' said Kate thoughtfully, 'and make it any size you wanted. It wouldn't be identical, because of the change in medium, but I think I could catch the essence of the picture. With that colouring I believe water-colour would work very well. But would that do?'

'Why don't you stay awhile and do some sketches so that we can see how it would work?' suggested Mrs Harcourt.

'Thank you,' said Kate. 'I'd like that.'

The bedroom to which she was shown had a wide casement window to the front of the house. Looking out, Kate could see down the long slope of the hill to where, at the bottom, the canal ran by. She would be able to see the boats passing. The white goat lifted its head and stared up towards the house. Kate felt sure it could see her.

The room was light and fresh with a faded rose-patterned rug on polished boards and a white candlewick quilt on the brass-railed bed.

Kate was puzzled. The house was substantial and everything about Giles had suggested the confidence of money. Yet, although Court Castle had a kind of old-fashioned style, it had a threadbare air, as though nothing had been replaced there for a very long time. Of course, this could be just the way the Harcourts preferred to live. Everything, though old, was cared for. Kate had heard that some old families clung to their past and refused to let modern convenience in.

It was certainly quite unlike the neat suburban villa on the edge of town in which Kate brought up. There had been no old silver, no valuable paintings, no leather-bound books, but if anything became worn Kate's mother fretted until it had been replaced by something neatly new.

In a way it was the very loving order of her parents' home which sent Kate wandering and seeking her bread and butter where she could find it. She loved her parents, but not their life-style. And they were proud of her, a late and only child, but puzzled to have produced an artist with a good deal of temperament and an independent mind.

She tidied herself and went downstairs where she found the lady of the house in the big kitchen rolling out pastry.

'Come and talk to me,' she invited, 'while I finish this pie for supper.'

Kate pulled up a pine chair to the big scrubbed kitchen table.

'Could you tell me something about your husband's mother?' she asked. 'It would help me to get the feel of things.'

'She was a great beauty, as you can see. Her husband loved her very much. She had a passion for roses and he made her rose gardens which were famous in their day. I'm afraid he neglected the family business to do it. But my husband never cared for the gardens and they were allowed to deteriorate.'

'What a shame,' said Kate. 'I love flowers.'

'Oh, Giles has made them lovely

71

again. He is so clever.'

'Is he — is Giles — at home today?'

'Oh no,' said Mary. She lined a pie-dish and, balancing it on one hand, deftly trimmed the edge with a sharp knife. 'Giles has gone to town on business. Of course, you know him quite well, don't you?'

'Not really,' said Kate. 'I only helped on the Rose Ann for one weekend.' She looked thoughtfully at Mary. 'I wonder — you seem very busy — could I be any help to you while I am here?'

'I expect you could,' said Mary, looking with satisfaction at her completed creation, 'but it doesn't seem fair, really. Margy helps — when she can be bothered,' she added vaguely. 'And of course Mrs Binns comes in to clean.'

She popped her pie in the oven, washed her hands at the kitchen sink, and took off her apron again.

'Let's go upstairs and find you a room for work. You won't want to paint in your bedroom.'

As they passed the picture above the half-landing it seemed to Kate to glow and she was very conscious of the beautiful serenity of the young woman and the skill of the artist who had given her such breathing life.

Mary opened a door across the passage from Kate's bedroom. A few pieces of furniture had been pushed against the walls and covered by cloths. The window was large, taking up half of the outside wall. Looking out Kate could see a wide lawn, a stone wall with an arch, a further wall, a line of tall evergreen Leylandii and distantly, over their tops, the misty blue edge of the moors.

'I'll get Mrs Binns to give it a good clean out in the morning,' said Mary. 'I know you'll have to have the original moved in here when you're working — if you decide to stay. But that will have to wait until Giles comes home so that he can move it for you. I expect you can make a few experimental sketches while its still in place?'

'Yes, of course. Thank you very much. This will be real luxury after some of the work places I've had while I've been on the road.'

'Good. Then I'll leave you to look round. Why don't you have a wander in the gardens? You'll like them, I think. You must excuse me now but I always have a little lie-down at this time of day,' and Mary Harcourt gave her a friendly smile and slipped out of the door.

'I'm going to like it here,' thought Kate to herself, looking round the large airy room with satisfaction. She peered under the furniture covers and was pleased to find an old oak desk with a sloping top which would be ideal to work on and a straight-backed chair to go with it. If the chest of drawers was pulled out and turned sideways and placed just there the big oil painting could be leant against it and would get just the right amount of light.

Already Kate's fingers were itching to start the preliminary pencil sketches. Why worry about Giles? She'd be working alone and the commission seemed to be for his mother rather than for him.

* * *

The sun had begun to move down the sky. A light breeze, rose-scented, soothed the sun-touched skin of her face and arms. She stood for a moment looking down the hill to where the canal ran like a silver streak. Once it would have been busy with work boats carrying goods and fuel. Now only an occasional holiday boat went by. She went round the side of the house and across the lawn, blue shadowed now, attracted by the arch in the stone wall.

Stepping through she found herself surrounded by roses. All round the walls, almost concealing the stones, grew bushes covered with flowers: clear pink, mauve-pink, blush-pink, crimson-purple, creamy-white, dark crimson. Some almost reached the top of the walls. Others were shorter, grading down to dwarf at the front of the borders. The tumult of fragrance was amazing.

In the centre, in a gravelled circle, stood a graceful stone figure, a woman in Grecian dress carrying an urn. A circular bench ran beneath so that a visitor might sit and enjoy the flowers looking in any direction.

Kate cupped a clear pink rose in her hand, bending her head to drink in the wonderful scent. The flower sepals were covered in furry green and Kate realised that this was a moss rose, a great favourite with the Victorians but not so often seen today. Looking round she noticed that other roses had the same distinctive form. It was a garden entirely stocked with moss roses.

'Hallo.'

'Oh!'

Kate jumped. She had not noticed

the girl, half concealed by the central statue, who was kneeling by a trug full of weeds, and working on the border with a hand-fork.

Kate went forward. The girl was wearing an old khaki man's shirt with sleeves rolled up as an overall. She got up as Kate approached and pushed floppy fair hair from her forehead leaving a grubby smudge. Her eyes were blue and she looked vaguely familiar, as if Kate had met her before. The girl wiped her hand down her shirt and held it out.

'I'm Margy, Giles' sister. You must be Kate Trevine, the travelling artist. I've heard about you.'

Kate took the proffered hand which was square and brown. Giles' sister! No wonder Roly had laughed at her when she'd complained to him of Giles' high-handed ways and wondered indignantly that Margy had put up with it.

'Well, she went off, didn't she?' he'd replied reasonably, 'that's why you're here.'

77

Just like Roly not to tell her the whole story. He and Giles had evidently been having a joke at her expense. Drat all men.

Margy was looking at her critically. 'You're pretty. Well — kind of. Giles didn't say.'

She looked a bit discontented. Kate was taken aback.

'Thank you. I think,' she said, 'that you're pretty — no kind of — if we're having that kind of conversation!'

At this the younger girl relaxed and looked more friendly.

'Is this one of the gardens your mother was telling me about? Made by your grandfather for your grandmother — the lady in the picture?'

'Yes — this is the moss rose garden. Doesn't it smell heavenly? It was a terrible mess but Giles remade it. He found old moss roses all over the country to plant in it.'

'Which garden is your favourite?'

'I think the white garden — come and see.'

Margy put her tools neatly into the trug and led Kate through another arch in the further wall. Here the air seemed hushed. The garden was circular and in the centre rose a dovecote with white fantail pigeons strutting on its roof. Over the wall tumbled hundreds of white rambler roses and the border was planted with white shrub roses, underplanted with white phlox, white delphiniums, white pinks and daisies.

But it wasn't all white. A low hedge of lavender attracted bees and butterflies and one or two of the rose bushes held flowers flushed with pink. A curved niche held a seat.

'Giles designed this?'

Kate was even more astonished. The artist in her knew that only someone with a deep feeling for colour and design could have created such a place.

'My grandfather did the original design,' said Margy, 'but Giles brought it back to life.'

She looked questioningly at Kate.

'Are you going to stay and do the

picture? Giles didn't think you would.'

'Oh, didn't he?' said Kate, knowing at once that she had quite decided to stay at Court Castle until she'd completed the commission.

# 6

Kate slept well and woke up next morning longing to get to work.

It was difficult to find a comfortable position from which to study the portrait. In the end she settled for a spot halfway across the landing. By tilting her head she could look up at the beautiful, serene lady. But she could only look. It wasn't going to be possible to make even the preliminary pencil sketches from here. She would have to wait until the picture had been taken down.

She looked carefully, starting at the top and letting her glance run downwards, head bending forwards, concentrating on detail. She did not hear someone come quietly up the stairs behind her.

The urge to move to try and get a better view became too much. She stepped backwards and stood heavily on that someone's toe.

'I'm so sorry I'm in your way,' said Giles courteously, 'but I'd be careful if I were you or you'll tumble down the stairs.'

'Oh! You startled me!' Shock made her sound cross. 'I wasn't expecting you!'

'I've only just got home. I thought I recognised the back of your neck from a previous occasion. There's something especially delightful about the back of your neck. The pretty way your hair curls . . . '

Kate blushed. She remembered vividly the feeling of his arms around her on her first attempt at working a lock.

He looked down at her quizzically. In fact it was the first time he had seen her that he was thinking of, as she worked diligently on the narrow-boat roses.

'You blush easily,' he remarked. 'I like it.'

Kate moved a bit further away. She'd always coloured up quickly. It was a great trial to her. She didn't like it mentioned and felt hotter than ever.

Taking pity on her embarrassment Giles looked instead at the portrait on the wall.

'Empress Josephine,' he said. 'I'm almost certain.'

'But — what do you mean — surely it's your grandmother?'

'The rose,' explained Giles. 'One of the Gallicas — a very old rose. Clear rose pink veined with deep pink. Beautiful.'

Kate looked again at the rose in the lady's lap.

'Yes. Those are the colours. I never thought that the rose was recognisable too and had a name.'

Giles was frowning.

'You can't work here. It's dangerous and anyway the light isn't good enough.'

'I'm only studying it and trying to see how it would work out in watercolour.'

'Watercolour?' He narrowed his eyes

at the picture. 'Yes. I can see it. I think you are right. So you've decided to take the job?'

'I . . . '

'Of course you have. And you'll want the picture moved. Where are you going to work?'

'Your mother found me an empty room on next floor. Looking out at the back.'

Giles nodded.

'I know the one. I'll just go and consult her and then we'll fix it all up.'

He flipped a finger through one of her red-gold curls and saw it curl back like a small spring.

'Pretty,' he murmured again, and smiled into her eyes.

She watched him go down the stairs with mixed feelings.

Today he was dressed in a summer-weight suit of dark material, worn with the crisp white shirt and plain sky-blue tie which echoed the colour of his eyes. With his thick fair hair brushed back to lie smoothly over his head he looked every inch the smart business man. She found the way he ordered her about intolerable.

And yet there was always the suggestion of an amused twinkle in his eyes and a quirk at the corner of his lips. Was he laughing at her? Not exactly, she felt. It was more as though he was appreciating a secret joke.

She went down the stairs and sat on a chair in the hall to wait. Soon Giles returned and with him was a boy who looked about seventeen.

'This is Mike . . . He works in the gardens with me.'

Mike grinned shyly. He wore his hair very short, his skin was fair and reddened by the sun, and though lanky and thin he looked strong.

'Pleased to meet you,' he said.

The two men fetched a step-ladder and between them carefully lowered the portrait, then carried it up the rest of the stairs and along the passage. Kate held the door open while they manoeuvred into the room and then explained where she wanted the picture placed.

'That's right,' she said, pleased that she had guessed so well where the light would fall. 'Thank you very much.'

'Okay, Mike. That's all for now,' said Giles.

The boy grinned and departed.

Giles looked at Kate.

'You will stay, won't you? We'll all be very disappointed if you don't.'

He no longer seemed to be laughing at some private joke but serious, even anxious.

Kate turned from studying the picture and saw the softened expression in the blue eyes as he looked at her. Wrestling with the large frame had made the fair hair flop over his forehead again and had streaked his face with dust. He no longer looked like the immaculate Smart Alec he had seemed at first sight.

'I expect so,' she said. 'Once I get started on something I have to finish.

To at least try and do it. I see what I want so clearly in my head.'

'I know,' he said. 'I feel the same.'

'Do you? Oh yes — the rose gardens.'

But just as Kate was feeling that they were in accord she realised that the humorous look had returned and she felt shut out and excluded. The victim of some silly joke.

'What's so funny,' she observed, turning away.

'Well,' he explained, 'it's not funny really, I suppose. But I think perhaps you have a wrong impression of me . . .'

'Do I?' said Kate, sounding indifferent. 'I don't think so.'

'So,' said Giles, 'you have decided to stay. Bed and board — as with Roly?'

He raised an eyebrow mockingly. At once Kate began to prickle again.

'Just so. *Exactly* as with Roly,' she said coldly.

Giles started to laugh.

'Oh Kate! You are funny! I don't

think what you think I think!'

'Just as well,' said Kate firmly. But she didn't believe him.

The rest of the morning she was busy making some preliminary sketches and thinking about colours. Giles did not appear for lunch and, after giving a hand with the washing up, Kate wandered out into the garden to take a break.

As she crossed the lawn Giles came through the arch in the wall. He was dressed now in thick brown cords worn with an open-necked shirt and his sturdy shoes were muddy. He looked pleased when he saw Kate and crossed the lawn towards her.

'Hallo,' she said, 'I thought you must have gone away again.'

'I often take sandwiches for lunch. Don't want to waste time. Come and see my roses.'

'I've seen them,' said Kate, 'and they are lovely. Especially the white garden.'

'No. I don't think you have,' said

Giles. 'The formal gardens are my grandfather's. *My* roses are further on. Come and see.'

Beyond the last wall of the formal gardens stood the long windbreak of tall dark Leylandii Kate had seen from her work room. A path led beside and then through the trees and there, beyond them, stretched a field that seemed to go on and on. It was filled with row after row of low bushes touched with colour — red, yellow, pink, orange and white.

'They're not quite at their best yet. Maiden roses reach their peak later than those in the gardens. Come and see them next month in their full glory.'

'You're a rose farmer!' exclaimed Kate.

'That's right,' he agreed, 'and it's hard work. Look!'

He held out his hands and she could see the thickened skin on the palms from digging and hoeing and the scratch marks where the fingers had been caught by thorns. She found herself wanting to take hold of his hands and gently touch the calluses. She thrust her own, instead, into the pockets of her jeans.

'Why didn't you tell me before?'

'I could see you had me down as a capitalist swine. I couldn't resist playing along. Roly could see the joke.'

'Roly isn't interested in anyone but himself,' said Kate. '*I* know that. And I suppose everyone else assumed that I knew. How silly of me.'

'No. Why was it? Come and sit down. I'm going to tell *you* a story.'

They sat on a rough plank bench and looked out over the rose fields. At one end were some outbuildings and Kate could see Mike in the distance industriously hoeing between rows. There was a heavy humming of bees. She turned towards Giles.

'Please tell me,' she said.

'I have to explain that you are right in your estimation of me in one respect. I *am* a business man. I have to be, for my father left the family in a pretty mess when he died. I need financial help and the Americans you met on the Rose Ann are — I hope — going to invest in our old English roses. Money for romance, you see.'

'They were nice people,' said Kate.

'This house, Harcourt Castle, was built by my great grandfather. He was very rich. He owned a textile mill in the town and he had an interest in the canal as well. He liked to be able to look down the hill and see the goods being transported one way and the coal the other.'

'The narrow boats would have been pulled by horses then, wouldn't they?' asked Kate, fascinated by the pictures conjured in her mind.

'That's right. But life plays tricks and his son, my grandfather, couldn't care less about any of it. He married the girl in the picture and led a careless, lazy life. Except for the rose gardens.

'Because my grandmother loved roses he made the gardens and they were some of the best of their kind.'

'I see. He spent money instead of making it.'

'My father tried. But his health was broken by serving in the Second World War. And by then there was no mill. There was little money. Only a big old house.'

'He could have sold it?' said Kate tentatively.

'Would you have sold it? Life has to be about more than bread and butter.

'When I was a boy I used to help him. It was his ambition to bring back the formal gardens to their full beauty. I became as hooked on roses as my grandmother had been. I went to agricultural college but just before I graduated my father died.'

'I'm sorry.'

'He hadn't been a fit man for a long time. I was walking alone in the gardens thinking about him when I realised what I wanted to do — but I'd do it in such a way that I'd make a living and be able to keep the house.'

It was almost as if the man beside her was melting into a mist and reforming into something quite different. She had thought him hard and unfeeling, bossy and money-orientated, on very little evidence. She was ashamed. She looked at him shyly and waved a hand at the field of flowers.

'You made all this from nothing?'

'It was a strip of farm land, pretty unpromising, too. But I raised some capital and got help to rotivate and feed and I've worked hard with my hands.

'But there is another side — advertising, selling, making contacts, and for that I do have another personna.'

'I remember,' said Kate with a grin.

He looked at her with obvious pleasure.

'I'm glad you've come, Kate. I hoped you would. I think you and I have a lot in common.'

She felt the all-too-ready colour begin to rise to her cheeks.

'I must get back,' she said, and got

quickly to her feet.

He was looking amused again. She wished he wouldn't. It made her feel diminished, somehow, as though he was looking at her as a light-hearted entertainment instead of as a real person.

He walked back to the house with her. They paused below the steps and looked down the slope to the canal which was catching the afternoon sun.

'I don't see,' said Kate, 'how you could afford to buy the Rose Ann if things were that bad?'

'I didn't buy her. She belonged to Barney, one of the last of the individual boat owners who plied for hire. My father let him keep her in our loading bay at the bottom of the hill. I used to play on her as a child. Barney and I were great pals. He left her to me. He knew I loved her. The doing up has taken years. And you,' he added, smiling down at her, 'have added the finishing touch!'

He put out a hand towards her hair

but Kate evaded it and ran up the steps. She felt confused but happy. Her mind was full of boats and mills and roses. All she wanted now was to get back to the serene company of her painted lady. Who didn't — who couldn't — laugh at her.

# 7

When Mary Harcourt fell off a stool trying to reach a top cupboard Kate was working upstairs. The crash was muffled by distance but she thought she heard a cry, parked her brushes and ran downstairs to the kitchen. The older woman was lying on the floor, a broken bag of sugar in her hand and the stool lying nearby.

Kate knelt down. Mary was looking very white but she said: 'Help me up, dear. I've been a bit silly and made rather a mess I'm afraid.'

Kate slid an arm behind Mary's shoulders and eased her into a sitting position.

'I'll be all right in a minute. I've got to get on with the evening meal.'

Kate was doubtful.

'I don't think you ought to try and do anything more. You look very shocked. I'll help you to the sofa in the drawing-room so that you can lie down. You could do with a rest and a cup of tea.'

'No, no. I'm all right.'

But when Mary was helped to stand up she was very rocky and found it hard just to get to a resting place.

Kate tucked her up under a rug and brought the tea.

'Now don't worry. Just tell me where things are and I'll get the supper.'

'It doesn't seem fair. You're here to work as an artist not a kitchen maid.'

'I said I'd be glad to help out when I came. I meant it. And now you really must lie still so please don't tire yourself arguing.'

Sugar is really nasty stuff to clear up and it took Kate some time to get the kitchen fit to work in. At first she had to go to and fro to ask where things were kept but soon Mary dozed off and Kate had to find things for herself.

It was funny how Margy never seemed to be about when there was extra work to be done. But she had said at lunch-time that she was going down to the village on her bike. Giles, of course, was busy on his rose farm.

Soon the vegetables were prepared and a hotpot was simmering on the stove. The surfaces had been scrubbed spotless and the air was warm and fragrant with the scent of herbs and bubbling stew.

Margy came back rather late in the afternoon. She peeped in at her sleeping mother, then sat in the kitchen with Kate. She seemed a bit subdued and Kate had the feeling that this came from some personal problem and was not solely due to her mother's accident.

Giles came in at last and went off to have a good clean-up and change his shirt. By the time he came down Mary was awake.

'Really I'm all right. I expect I'm a little bit bruised but that's all. Yes — I will see the doctor in the morning if there's any doubt. Don't fuss, my dears. I'll just have an early night.'

'Good idea,' said Giles, as he scooped his mother up in his arms and carried her, laughing and protesting, up the stairs.

It seemed to be Kate's fate to end up doing the domestic chores. But this was different from skivvying on the Rose Ann.

She spread a blue checked cotton cloth on the wide deal table and took her seat opposite Giles. He stacked his plate with potatoes and made a hearty meal. Kate found that it gave her great satisfaction to see him eating the food she had prepared.

Margy did not eat much. She did not show the appetite one would expect from a young woman who had just been on a long cycle ride. She did not say much either and left the table early without offering to stay and wash up.

Giles finished his meal with a slice of cold apple pie and several slices of bread and cheese.

Then he sat back with an air of satisfaction.

'That was very good,' he said. 'Thanks, Kate. Where's that pesky sister of mine gone?' He stood up and stretched. 'I'll help with the dishes.'

'There's no need. You've been working hard all day.'

'But I'd like to.'

He looked round for a tea-towel as Kate filled a bowl with hot water.

'What is the matter with Margy?' asked Kate, her hands busy with dishes and mop.

'Boredom, I should think,' said Giles. 'She did a course at college so that she can do the books for me but that's not enough. She ought to get a proper job. She's so much younger than I am that I can't help worrying about her. There's plenty to do in the house and garden and mother loves her company but . . .'

'But at her age she needs a bit of fun.'

'She gets that by taking off into town,' said Giles ruefully. 'I wish she had something she really wanted to do.

100

That's where you're so lucky. You have your bent.'

'That's true in a way,' said Kate thoughtfully, 'but not altogether. I haven't yet worked out how to please myself *and* earn a living. In that respect you're the lucky one. It doesn't matter how hard one works, does it, if one is doing something one cares about?'

\* \* \*

The next day Mary was back on her feet. Giles insisted on running her down to the village in his old car to see the doctor although his mother said it made her feel foolish.

'Goodness, it was only a little tumble!' she protested.

Kate was able to get back to her painting.

She had drawn the slender cupped hands holding the rose and was experimenting with the colours, veining the petals with the deeper pink. Somehow it didn't look quite right.

101

She wished Giles was there so that she could ask his advice. There was a soft knock on the door. Kate's heart jumped.

But when the door opened it was Margy who stood there.

'Come in,' said Kate in a friendly voice, 'perhaps you can help me.'

Of course it could not possibly have been Giles. It had been a foolish thought.

Margy moved hesitantly into the room. She was wearing a blue cotton skirt with a frilled white blouse this morning. She looked very pretty but her face was morose, lips turning down at the corners and a little frown between her brows.

'How can I help?'

Kate gestured at her sketch block.

'This rose — have I got it right?'

Margy glanced at it and looked bored.

'Oh, roses. I'm sick of roses.'

She moved restlessly about the room, finally standing just where she blocked off the light. Kate resigned herself. She put down her brush.

'What is it? You seem fed up?'

'I went to see Roly when I was out yesterday,' said the other girl abruptly. 'You know him, don't you?'

'Yes. Very well.'

'I mean — you knew him before? Not just on the Rose Ann?'

'We were at art college together.'

'Giles met him in a pub. He was drinking too much and hadn't got a job. Giles hired him to run the Rose Ann. He's jolly good at it.'

'Yes. I could see that.'

Margy twisted her fingers together.

'The trouble is — he won't take me seriously! He says it wouldn't be right to play games with Giles' little sister when he owes Giles so much. He holds me off — and I *love* him, Kate!'

This showed an unexpected strength of mind on Roly's part. Kate was impressed. Margy was a very attractive young woman and must have been throwing herself at Roly in no uncertain manner.

'Have you spoken to Giles about this?' she asked cautiously.

'Yes. I have. He just laughs. *He* thinks I'm only keen on Roly because he's the only man around but its *not* that. I see plenty of others when I go and stay with my friends in town and go to discos and things. But they're not like Roly. He's different. He's special.'

Kate looked at the girl in some dismay. She remembered very well how charming Roly could be. And now there was the added glamour of his casual free life on the narrow boat. She thought that Giles might well have a point.

She hesitated, then: 'Are you hoping he will ask you to marry him, Margy?'

Margy's face lit up.

'If only he would! I wouldn't mind living in a garret while he struggled to become known as a great painter!'

'Ah — but would you mind living

in a neat little house while Roly went to work from nine till five?'

Margy stamped her foot.

'You're just like Giles! You don't believe I love Roly! But I do — I do! It's not just a silly dream! I'd want to be with him anywhere!'

'The thing is — I do know Roly pretty well and he's not much of a one for taking responsibility. He always used to say he wanted to be free. You might be content but would Roly?'

'You're stupid!' cried Margy furiously. 'I thought you'd be different and understand. He doesn't have to marry me if he's hung up on freedom but he won't — he won't — because of Giles!'

She gave an angry sob.

'I'm sorry — I didn't mean to upset you . . . ' but Margy was gone, blue skirts swirling as she passed. The jar of discoloured paint water fell over and soaked the Empress Josephine so that her colours ran. The sketch was ruined.

★ ★ ★

Margy ran out of the house and down the terrace. She pushed open the small iron gate and was out in the buttercup strewn meadow. Nancy, the white goat, lifted her head and trotted across to see her mistress, bleating in a welcoming way.

Margy put her arms round the animal's rough white neck and buried her face in its odorous fur.

'You're the only friend I've got,' she said.

The white goat bleated again and started to chew at the collar of Margy's blouse.

This made the girl laugh and she pushed the animal away and rubbed the top of its head. The sun shone and down below the canal lay straight and shining. What should she do? Roly had made it plain that she was welcome to visit the Rose Ann whenever she wished. He had also given her the kindest, most brotherly kiss, and told

106

her that she's soon get over wanting anything more from him.

Kate had been no help. She had thought that Kate, once she realised that Margy was serious, would offer to act as an intermediary. Roly was her friend.

Why had Kate been so damping? Could it be that she had an interest there herself? She must have been living on the boat with Roly for at least a week. Kate with her red hair and green eyes with whom he had background and ambitions in common. Was it likely that they had been together for all that time and nothing had happened?

\* \* \*

Kate, meanwhile, scrumpled up the soggy paper and started again. It hadn't been right, anyway.

She thought that she had probably handled the conversation badly but it had come out of the blue, she hadn't been expecting intimate confidences from Giles' sister, and she had simply told what she believed to be the truth.

Concentrating on her work she tried to put Margy and her problems out of her mind. After all, she hardly knew these people. This was just a stop on her travels. Perhaps a bit longer than some but soon she would be on her way again.

She would have been very surprised if she could have heard the dark suspicions that Margy was breathing into the hairy ear of the white goat.

# 8

'Did Giles tell you that we're having the Americans' grand-daughter to stay?' asked Mary over lunch. 'It seems she goes to school over here and the Mertons don't want to take her with them all the time. They fancy a romantic spell by themselves in Paris.'

'Another woman,' groaned Margy. 'This place is getting to be a harem — or possibly a nunnery would be more like it!'

'She's only thirteen,' objected Mary. 'Only a child. I'm sure she won't be any trouble.'

* * *

It was a sunny afternoon. Kate sat on a rock at the top of the field painting a quick watercolour sketch of the canal below. The goat stood nearby looking friendly and interested.

She heard Giles' car sweep round the house to the front door and stop. She put down her sketchbook and got up to look. A little breeze caught the page on which she had been working so that it waved in the air.

The goat moved closer. The paper stopped waving. The goat chewed steadily with a gleam of appreciation in her eye.

Kate turned round.

'Oh no! You wretched creature!'

It seemed that her sketches were fated to come to an untimely end. Twice they had been destroyed. Would there be a third time?

She gathered up her things and climbed the terrace. A girl was standing looking up at the house. Her hair was toffee-coloured, short and shiny and her eyes were grey. Her stance was solid and determined.

'I don't call that a castle,' she said disparagingly. 'I thought it would be a proper castle, you know, real old.'

'Sorry,' said Giles with a grin. 'The nearest we have of that kind of thing is Brindale Fort. That's a right old ruin.'

'Where's that?'

'Up on the moors. Perhaps I'll take you there one day if you're interested. Let me introduce you. This is Kate, who is an artist.'

The girl held out a hand.

'Hi! I'm Tamsin. Not Tammy. Not Tam. Tamsin.'

'Hello, Tamsin,' said Kate. 'I'll remember.'

★ ★ ★

Tamsin made herself at home very quickly. She was used to coping in strange places. Her parents were busy professional people and Tamsin got dumped around quite often. She had been disappointed but not surprised when her grandparents hadn't taken her to France. She looked forward to being with them later in the holiday but meanwhile she would amuse herself with whatever came to hand.

This turned out to be mainly Giles. Tamsin spent a lot of time helping out with the roses. Fetching and carrying, hoeing and raking, chatting to Giles and Mike. Fortunately the weather stayed fine so apart from having to cater for an extra appetite, a young and hearty one, she did not make a lot of difference to day-to-day living.

'That child's got a crush on Giles,' said Margy, 'what a bore.'

'It won't do her any harm,' said her mother firmly. 'She'd be bound to have a crush on someone, she's just the age. And even today American girls are more precocious than English ones.'

'The atmosphere in this place,' said Margy gloomily, 'is beginning to get me down, I think I'll be off to stay with Jill and Amy again soon.'

She wandered away looking fed up.

'Will you take me to see Brindale Fort, Giles?'

Giles was in the wooden shed he used as an office, frowning down at a sheaf of orders. Tamsin leaned against his shoulder. She felt a wonderful shivery feeling down her arm and sighed ecstatically.

Giles moved his glance from the papers and caught the full force of a melting gaze from the great grey eyes. He was getting just a little tired of all this puppy-like adoration. It was a problem. He didn't want to hurt Tamsin's feelings — she was very young and a guest in his home — but it was beginning to be a nuisance. Everywhere he went on the rose farm Tamsin tagged him, leaping to fetch him anything she thought he wanted, trying to anticipate his every wish. And fixing him with that gooey sheep's-eyes look that was causing Mike to give him some very peculiar glances.

113

He moved a little away, so that Tamsin had to straighten up, trying to make it seem like a natural movement and not like a rebuff.

'I'm sorry, Tamsin,' he said as gently as possible, 'it's too late to go today and I have to go into town on business.'

'Can I come into town with you?' asked Tamsin eagerly.

'No. I'm afraid not. I'm spending a long time with my accountant.'

'But I could look round the town by myself,' argued Tamsin. 'I wouldn't be a trouble.'

Giles hesitated. If he could have been sure how long his business would take he might have given in. But he was responsible for the child to the Mertons and knew himself well enough to know that once he got to grips with money problems he might well forget her altogether.

'Not this time. I've really got too much on my mind. Why don't you go and find Mike? I'm sure he'd like some help.'

Tamsin's mouth drooped and she went off slowly, dragging her feet on the hard dirt floor.

* * *

Kate had got the feel of her work and was painting quickly now. The rose lay across the pale curved hands, the creamy shoulders rose from a cloud of seagreen gauze, the eyes were not really blue, they seemed to reflect the colour of the gown with lights of aquamarine.

She felt inside herself the rising sense of excitement which came when work was going well. She thought that she had successfully caught the serenity of the lady's expression, the feeling the picture gave of someone who felt secure in love — the rose in her hands a gift from her lover.

Soon she would have finished and be free to leave Court Castle. Free to take up again her wandering life where each day might bring a new adventure. It was time to go — before wrenching herself away became an anguish. Because she knew too well that it wasn't only Tamsin who was becoming enmeshed in feelings that were not returned.

'And,' thought Kate to herself, 'I'm old enough to know better!'

When she cleaned her brushes that day and stood back to look at her copy she felt elevated by the feeling that she had done well. But, at the same time, found herself curiously envying the calm certainty of the lovely lady's demeanour. Would she ever feel like that? Wrapped in reciprocated love?

It was not her custom to use her workroom in the afternoons for the light was different and that would not do. But there were many other things that she wanted to paint while she was still here. Today she took her sketching things along to the white garden.

Giles, coming through an arch, paused for a while to watch. She sat on the stone bench in the alcove, framed by trailing white roses, her head bent over her work, the red-gold curls tumbling over her forehead. Because the day was so hot she had changed into a cool cotton dress, loose and clinging, patterned with pastel flowers. The white pigeons cooed and strutted.

She looked so right there. As if the niche in the wall had been waiting for her, the goddess of the garden.

He gave a little laugh and a shrug. It wasn't like him to indulge in sentimental imagery. He walked forwards.

Kate looked up and smiled.

'Hello, Giles. On your own? Where's your shadow today?'

'My? Oh! You mean Tamsin! I think . . . ' he looked round cautiously, 'I *think* she's busy helping Mike. Free at last! May I sit down?'

'Of course.'

Kate shifted along.

He sat beside her and looked at her work.

'Mm. You've got the feeling of this place beautifully. All cool and secluded.

You have a real talent for flowers. How are you getting along with my grandmother?'

'I think — I really think I've managed to transfer her convincingly. I hope your mother will be pleased.'

'You mean you've finished?'

Giles felt a sinking sensation.

'Except for the odd touch.'

'So you'll be leaving us?'

'Once a job is finished I'm on my way. There's nothing to stay for.'

He slid an arm round her shoulders and turned her to face him.

'Isn't there, Kate?'

He was looking a query, half mocking and half rueful.

'I believe I could find you something to stay for.'

His arm across her shoulders felt hot and heavy. She wanted to shrug it off yet was frozen with the fear of making a wrong move.

What did he mean? Did he feel the same attraction as she did or was he reacting automatically to the man and girl alone situation?

Giles was thinking: 'Damn! It's too soon — it's too soon. We need more time.' but he could not resist temptation. He drew Kate towards him so that her head rested against his shoulder, lifted her chin so that her face was tilted towards him, and kissed her on the mouth. Her skin was scented with roses and summer and her lips were soft as ripe strawberries. He wanted to crush in his arms and keep her there for ever but resolutely put her away.

Kate felt giddy. She would not have believed that such a slight caress could have sent such a wave of sweetness washing through her body. She hardly knew the man. She must keep her head.

She ran a hand over her tousled curls.

'What was that for?' she asked.

'It was 'thank you for being here' and 'don't go away' and 'I'm glad I met you' and — oh! — all kinds of things which must wait for another day.'

'I see,' she said, 'only there won't be another day, will there?'

'There must be, Kate. I have to be away on business again tomorrow. Don't go before I come back.'

Kate gathered her things together and put them in the linen satchel she carried slung over one shoulder. She looked at Giles.

'I *can't* stay,' she said, 'you know that. Your mother employed me to do a particular job and I've done it. I've loved being here — I like you all and you've made me very welcome. But . . . '

'But you have your own life to lead. Yes — I do see that. But supposing I could keep you working? Would you stay then?'

'Ah. But it would have to be real. Something that only I could do.'

They walked together towards the house. He smiled down at her and their glances met, each telling the same story. There was something there waiting in the wings — something that could be very good.

But Giles had guessed wrong when he imagined that Tamsin was safely occupied working with Mike. Soon after he had left the rose fields she had made an excuse and slipped away after him. Aware by now that Giles, though he tried to conceal it, was irritated at being followed, Tamsin kept some way behind and peeped cautiously round the arch.

She saw Giles take a seat beside Kate and drew back. A curtain of roses hung down between the arch and the bench in the niche and Tamsin was able to see without being seen.

She saw Giles' arm go round Kate's shoulders. She saw him draw Kate to him. She saw him bend and kiss.

And such a storm of despair and fury shook her that she almost cried out. Almost dashed from her hiding place, beat on Giles' broad back with clenched fists, hung on his arm trying to drag it away from her rival.

For that was how she saw the older girl; while at the same time knowing that against Kate's maturity she had no weapon. She was only a child. Judged only a child by all the adults while inside raged passions as strong as any she would ever feel, though — and she could not believe this — not as lasting.

She turned and fled. She could see Mike in the distance still working so turned the other way, ran along the line of sheltering evergreens until she came to a spot where two trees formed a green cave. Here she crept in and lay curled on the bed of dry needles, sobbing and sobbing with the aromatic scent of the cypress all around.

'It's not fair; it's not fair. Nobody loves me.'

At supper Tamsin was pale and silent. She ate very little and stared down at her plate, pushing her food about.

Mary was worried.

'Are you all right, Tamsin? Do you

have a headache? It was very hot today and you will work out in the fields without a sun hat.'

Tamsin looked up and smiled wanly.

'My head does ache a little. Do you mind if I go to bed now?'

'Of course, dear. I'll bring you up an asprin.'

After Tamsin had gone Mary said: 'I do hope the child isn't sickening. It's so worrying being responsible for someones else's young.'

# 9

Tamsin did not appear for breakfast next morning. Margy was still moody. Giles was wearing a tie and a sober suit and went off soon after the meal.

Margy put down her empty coffee cup and hurried after him.

'Wait for me, Giles! I'd like a lift into town.'

Mary and Kate looked at each other ruefully.

'Never mind,' said Kate, 'I'll give you a hand. I've almost finished the picture. I'd like to show it to you later today.'

Together they cleaned up the kitchen and washed and dried the dishes.

'I think I'll just take a tray up to Tamsin and make sure she's all right. She did look peaky yesterday,' said Mary. 'It isn't like her not to eat.'

Kate also went upstairs to her

workroom. She felt happy about her work and keen to see it again. She pushed open the door. For a moment she stood still, puzzled. The room was full of bright morning light, the original portrait leant against the chest of drawers, the furniture was all in its usual place, but something was wrong.

She had left the copy, still taped to its board and covered with a layer of light tissue as protection, on the sloping surface of the old writing desk. As she walked forwards she could see that though the board was still there the picture was not. It had been ripped from its moorings, torn, scrumpled and thrown on the floor.

A strange feeling of unreality came over Kate. It seemed incredible that anyone could be so cruel. She felt the colour drain out of her face and had to put out a hand and grasp the back of the tall wooden chair. She felt sick and giddy.

Who had done it — who had destroyed the hours of careful work which had given her so much pleasure? At first her thoughts flew to Margy and the incident of the spilt paint water and the spoiled sketch. But that had been an accident while this was deliberate. Whoever had done it had wanted to hurt.

Mechanically Kate tidied up, picked up the pieces of paper and smoothed them out. She laid them on the board. And the lady gazed calmly back from the jigsaw of lines and edges. Somehow it helped to steady Kate. She gathered the bits together and put them into a folder. Then she left the room, quietly shutting the door behind her. She leant for a moment against the wall, taking deep breaths, and then went downstairs.

Mary came out of the drawing-room. She looked troubled.

'Have you seen Tamsin? I took her up some breakfast but she wasn't there. She seems to have dressed and gone out early. Why should she do that?'

Tamsin! But why would Tamsin

destroy her picture? Kate had always got on well with the child. Had thought they were friends. But a picture came into her mind of Giles smiling down and Tamsin gazing up at him adoringly.

She pushed it aside. The important thing now was to take the worry from Mary's face and the distress from her eyes. She laid a hand on the older woman's arm.

'I expect she's up on the rose farm with Mike,' she said. 'I'll go and see.'

Mike leaned on his hoe and looked thoughtful.

'I did see Tamsin but it was a while back as I was coming in to work. She was heading up the footpath over there.'

They both turned and looked. The footpath led up a hillside where sheep grazed. Beyond loomed the misty blue of the far-off moors.

'Mike! Good heavens! She must be trying to walk to Brinsdale Fort! She's been nagging Giles to take her.'

'She has that,' agreed Mike, 'and it's just the sort of spunky thing she would do.'

'Oh dear! And Giles has gone off in the car. She'll never get there and back. I must go after her. Where's Margy's bike?'

'In the shed over there. Go down to the village — you'll see the fort signposted.'

'Tell Mrs Harcourt,' called Kate as she ran over to the shed and pulled out the bicycle.

She stopped in the village to fill her pockets with chocolate from the small post-office-cum-store.

There were few cars and Kate found she was enjoying the ride; the only sounds the occasional bleat from a sheep or the whirring wings of a startled partridge.

Presently the road became steeper and she had to work really hard. The air got cooler and the sky darkened. Purple clouds were building up behind the moors.

At last she could see the fort. In the distance it looked black against the rise behind. It was very much a ruin: two broken towers and a length of crumbling wall. A rocky track led there from the road. Kate got off and pushed the bike along it. The purple clouds were advancing. There was a flash of sheet lightening which illuminated the scene with an eerie glow. Kate's heart stood still.

Halfway across the ancient wall, and two thirds of the way up, clung a small figure in a turquoise sweater, spread-eagled on the rough surface and seemingly frozen with fear. There was a crash as thunder rolled and a few spots of heavy rain were cold as they hit Kate's cheeks. Then came a frightened cry, almost like a wild bird.

'Tamsin!' Kate cried back inside herself but she did not shout it aloud for fear of startling the petrified child. She flung down the bicycle and raced forwards.

The ruin was surrounded by an

iron fence and the iron gate had a padlock and chain. But these were only loosely hitched over the gatepost and easily lifted so that the gate could be pushed open.

Kate moved cautiously up to the bottom of the wall. She stepped over a piece of old white board and turned it over with one foot. It read in damaged letters: 'Danger. Falling stones.'

When she was directly below the climber Kate called up.

'Tamsin. It's me — Kate. Are you all right?'

The voice that answered was strained and faint.

'I'm stuck. I can't move.'

Kate took off her anorak and dumped it on the grass.

'Hang on. I'm coming up,' she called.

There was another flash, nearer this time, and the roll of thunder seemed right overhead. Rain was coming harder, making the stones of the fort wet and slippery. Kate climbed with care, feeling for holds with her hands and feet. At last she was clinging to the wall alongside of Tamsin and could see the girl's white face and widened eyes.

'Don't look down,' she said, 'though it's not really all that far. I'm going to find you new holds and move you bit by bit. You must trust me. Are your feet secure?'

'Yes. But I can't move,' gasped Tamsin.

'You can. I'll help you.'

Kate felt until she found a firm crevice then took Tamsin's nearest hand in hers.

'I've got you.' she said. 'You are quite safe.' and guided her hand until Tamsin's fingers gripped the new hold. Reaching across to move the girl's other hand was more difficult but the warmth of her body pressing on Tamsin's back seemed to help pass on reassurance.

'Now I'll do the same for your feet.'

'No — no — I'll slip!'

There was a new panic in the cry.

131

'No you won't because I won't let you,' said Kate firmly.

With great care and making sure that Tamsin could feel her grip she lowered the feet one at a time to new and safe positions. And when she had done this Tamsin's panic went as suddenly as it had come.

'I'm all right now!' she exclaimed, 'don't touch me any more!' and, scrambling and scrabbling she inched her way down until she could drop safely to the ground.

The rain had passed over leaving the walls of the fort damp and shiny. Thunder rumbled distantly now. And there was a new sound, the engine of an approaching car.

It stopped. There was a crunch of footsteps and Tamsin crying: 'Giles! Giles! You came to find me! I knew that you would come!'

Kate looked round and the weight of her body swung across on to one hand. Her fingers grasped strongly but a stone moved and suddenly broke away. For a moment she hung there, fighting for balance but in vain. She fell heavily and lay in a crumpled heap at the foot of the wall.

Giles pushed Tamsin to one side and leaped forwards; and then he was kneeling in the damp grass at Kate's side. She opened her eyes. Jackdaws cried and flew across a sky now blue.

'I'm all right,' she gasped, 'just a bit giddy. I know how to fall.'

It seemed quite natural that Giles should be there; quite natural that his arms lifted her gently and he strode back towards the car.

'You don't need to carry me,' she protested, 'I can walk.'

'Don't be silly,' he retorted.

Tamsin trotted along behind. As Giles lowered Kate on to the car seat she said urgently: 'Margy's bike. I borrowed it without asking. I must . . .'

She tried to struggle out but was pushed firmly back.

'It can wait,' said Giles. 'I'll fetch it later.'

'My dear,' said Mary when they arrived back home, 'now it's your turn to stay in bed. You may well be suffering from shock.'

And indeed Kate was glad to be tucked up with a hot water bottle and a warm drink. The long up-hill bicycle ride, the unnerving climb, and the final tumble had combined to make her very tired. The world seemed to be whirling slowly round her in a strange manner. Warmth crept into her limbs bringing sweet relaxation. Very soon she sank into a deep sleep.

It was getting towards dusk when she woke. Outside in the garden a song thrush was fluting its repetitive song. The scent of a yellow climbing rose blew in through the open window on the evening breeze.

There was a light knock on the door. Kate pulled herself up on her pillow.

'Come in,' she called.

The door opened and Tamsin came

in, carefully carrying a tray on which stood a covered dish and the air filled with the delectable smell of vegetable soup. Kate sniffed appreciatively and realised that she was very hungry. Tamsin placed the tray on the bedside table.

'Thanks,' said Kate, smiling. 'How are you, Tamsin? You got just as cold and wet as I did even though you didn't tumble.'

'I'm all right,' said Tamsin, gruffly. 'They did try to make me lie down but I couldn't stand it.'

'Of course,' said Kate ruefully, 'you are younger than I am.'

Tamsin shifted from one foot to another then burst out: 'I'm sorry, Kate. I spoilt your painting. I was mad as a coyote, I guess.'

'I thought it must have been you,' said Kate. 'But why? Aren't we friends?'

Tamsin had flushed a fiery red.

'I saw Giles kiss you,' she blurted out. 'I was jealous.'

'Why, you poor kid,' said Kate,

135

stretching out her hand. 'You shouldn't have minded about that. It was just one of those things. It didn't mean anything. I'm just nearer his age — and I was there!'

'I know,' muttered Tamsin, 'and I don't mind now. But at the time . . . I'm truly sorry, Kate.'

Kate took the girl's hand and gave it a warm squeeze.

'Don't worry. It's all in the past. I can paint the lady again. No problem.'

'Can you?' said Tamsin eagerly. 'I'm so glad.'

'Now,' said Kate, 'for goodness sake pass me that soup or I'll go into a decline from starvation!'

The soup was good. Tamsin took the empty bowl and went away. Kate was lying back, warmed and comfortable, when there came another knock at the door. This time it was Giles.

'How are you, Kate? Still feeling shaken?'

She shook her head. He sat down on the end of the bed and smiled at her. She smiled back, shyly. His blue eyes crinkled at the corners and she had the oddest notion that the song of the thrush had become that of the nightingale.

'I heard about the picture being torn up. That was rotten for you. All that work destroyed. It was that little rat Tamsin, wasn't it?'

'Yes. But Giles, don't be cross with her. She's really very lonely under that smartypants American exterior. She filled the gap by forming this terrific crush on you.'

'Don't I know it!'

'She must have been following you, she saw you — me — in the white rose garden.' Kate's voice faltered. She didn't know quite how to put it.

'She saw me kiss you,' said Giles.

'Yes. I see. So she went and tore up your painting. There's teenage passion for you.'

'She didn't stop to think,' urged Kate. 'She just wanted to vent her feelings on something. And to hurt me, of course. She's apologised now. In fact I get the impression that being frozen with fright on a crumbling wall in a thunderstorm has washed her quite clean of overheated feelings.'

'Right. I forgive her if you do. I know she's only a child. And she's done me a favour.'

'What's that?'

'Why — you'll have to stay on and do the painting all over again. It's an ill wind, etc!'

'So I shall,' said Kate.

He got up from the bed. On the way to the door he paused.

'Tell me, Kate, what do you imagine happened to that itinerant painter of roses and castles of yours?'

'Why, I've always thought that he fell in love with a local girl, married and settled down near the canal.'

'Sensible fellow,' said Giles.

# 10

Kate was happy. She sang at her work. It wasn't going to be too difficult, after all, to copy the portrait again. At first, despite her kind assurance to Tamsin, she had thought that she couldn't, that all the fire and dedication had gone. But soon she was absorbed and her fingers, delicately holding the brush, flew across the paper.

The room was quiet except for Kate's voice which rose, light and melodious, so that it seemed a drift of traditional English folksong hung like vapour below the ceiling.

Outside a breeze had got up and the window was shut to prevent dust and papers from blowing about. But for Kate there was no barrier. Out there, across the swaying line of dark trees, Giles was working among his roses. She imagined him, fair hair ruffled, blue shirt sleeves rolled up, concentrating on his precious plants. As she must concentrate on *her* work.

She understood now, how the lady in the picture had felt. For a moment, cradled in Giles' arms as he carried her to the car, she had known what it was to be loved and protected. She smiled to herself. She could still feel his arms around her. There had been that in his face, a look of urgent anxiety as he had looked down at her lying below the fort wall, and then the brightening with relief when she spoke.

Her thoughts went back to the white garden. She remembered how he had tilted her face up to his, there among the roses, and how, caught unaware, her body had responded.

He had said something about finding her some more work. What could it be? Perhaps he would suggest that she cleaned and restored those murky Victorian landscapes?

Certainly she could do it but without the enthusiasm which she felt for the delightful Twenties lady. And if she stayed on she would see more of Giles. Her heart moved at the thought.

The light changed as the sun outside rose higher into the sky. It was time to get ready for lunch. Back in her bedroom Kate ran a comb through her curls and changed the apple green painter's smock she wore for work for a light wool sweater and skirt in the same colour. The wind was beating on the other side of the house so she was able to open her window. She leaned out below the nodding yellow roses and took a deep breath of fresh air, scented, as always around Court Castle, with the scent of many flowers.

The sound of a car engine made her turn her head. Round the corner from the left swept the golden sports car and pulled up on the semi-circular gravel patch before the main door.

Rowenda got out and walked round the car. Her hair was tied up in a pink kerchief, fastened at the back like an Italian grape-picker, the ends flicking in the breeze. She wore a matching high-necked sweater, loose and floppy, below which her legs looked endlessly long and slim.

Kate drew back. As she did so Giles came down the steps. He was dressed, not as she had imagined for working in the fields, but in the smart suit he had worn when she first met him by the canal. Looking down from above Kate could not see their faces but heard Rowenda's clear voice cry: 'Darling!' and saw the other girl's arms go out and round Giles' neck. He bent and kissed her.

They walked back to the car with Giles' arm about the visitor's waist. She slipped into the passenger seat and Giles took the wheel. They were both laughing. The car reversed neatly, turned, and purred away round the corner.

Kate shut the window. She was pale and trembly with shock. It was as though she had been punched very hard over the heart. How could she have been so stupid? To let a man she knew so little get under her skin in such a way. As if she hadn't learned her lesson long ago.

He'd been playing with her. All the time her first impression had been right. He might not be the rich business man she had imagined yet, but he was on his way. In his slick suit, with his rich American backers, he was in his right place in that showy car with that smart girl. What would he want with a vagrant artist who was happy just sitting in a field with a goat?

Though Giles spent a great deal of his life tilling the soil and working among his roses he must be pretty tough to keep all this up and make it prosper. He had been very young to take over; to become the kingpin of the family machine. It was not only hard labour with hands and arms and back that was needed to keep up this large old house and wring money from the earth but brains and business acumen. The ruthless streak she had sensed on their first meeting must be there. He knew how to hide it when it did not suit to have it seen.

Kate was desolate. The Giles she thought she knew had faded away in a moment.

She chatted as cheerfully as she could to Tamsin and Mary over lunch and helped to clear away and wash up as usual.

Mary was worrying about Margy.

'I wish she wouldn't stay away so long without ringing. I know she's grown-up now and I ought to let go. If she had a life of her own — but she's not *happy*. She was always so impulsive as a child. And I don't like those friends of hers.'

'She's bored, isn't she?' said Kate. (Tamsin had slipped away before the washing-up commenced.)

'Yes,' said Mary. 'Giles has offered to find her a flat in town if she wants to get a job there but she won't go. It's troubling.'

Kate sank back on the squashy

cushions of the drawing-room sofa. The old white cat slept by her side making a warm path against her thigh. It opened one pale green eye a slit but sank back into slumber, purring heavily, as Kate's hand caressed its head. There was comfort in the living presence beneath the silken fur. Kate laid her head back and tried to relax.

Mary Harcourt, coming in with the coffee, was concerned that the red-gold curls framed such a pale face. The chink of china as it was set down on a small table made Kate sit up and smile, rather tremulously.

'What is it, Kate? You don't look well. Are you still feeling shaken from your fall? Perhaps you shouldn't work so hard so soon.'

'No, no. I'm all right really. It's just that — I really have to think about moving on. It's been lovely staying here — I've enjoyed it so much — but the summer is passing, the picture is nearly finished, and I must find another job.'

'Oh no!' exclaimed Mary, 'surely

not yet? It's been such fun having you here.'

'It has been quite my best job,' said Kate, 'and I shall miss you. But when a job's done it's done and it is best to go quickly.'

★ ★ ★

The wind had dropped. The white goat grazed peacefully. Down below the canal glittered in the afternoon sun. To Kate's surprise a narrow boat was moored in the private loading bay at the bottom of the slope. It looked like the Rose Ann.

As she watched a figure disembarked and began to climb the path. A distant bark made the white goat raise its head and stare with yellow eyes towards the intruder. The figure came nearer — yes — it was Roly! And that faint brown blur on the cabin top must be Ailsa grumbling at being deserted.

Roly pushed open the small iron gate and mounted the steps between

146

the terraced roses.

'Hallo, Kate. Have you seen Margy?'

'I'm afraid she's away again, Roly. Did you want her especially for something?'

'Not especially. Or not more especially than usual. She hasn't been round lately. I wondered if she'd gone away altogether. Found a job at last. Just curious, that's all.'

'Come in and see Mary,' said Kate taking him by the arm and pushing him towards the front door.

'Well — if it's no bother . . . ' said Roly, a little reluctantly. 'I don't want to be a nuisance.'

But Mary was plainly delighted to see him and poured out all her worries about Margy in a relieved rush.

'She usually *rings* you see, because she knows I get lonely. But I suppose she thinks that with Kate and Tamsin here I'm all right. I can't help worrying, I don't know why, but those friends of hers lead such *different* lives.'

Roly listened with a frown. Then he

said: 'Don't fret so, Mrs Harcourt. I know where she hangs out. I'll fetch her home.'

* * *

Margy was out on the small circular dance floor. Flashing strobe lights passed across her face turning it first green, then blue, then white. She danced alone, eyes huge and dark, scarcely seeing the many faces in the surrounding shadow. Her fair hair tossed and swung, as did the large gold ear-rings pendant from her ears. A thick gold chain bounced over the low-cut black sweater above the tight black skirt.

Roly paused just inside the door to watch. He hated to see Margy looking like that. As if she was moving in some private hell. There was nothing of enjoyment in her face. The lights moved over her. The music beat heavily on. Roly started forwards and seized Margy by the wrists.

'Come on,' he said, 'I'm taking you out of this!'

The blankness left the girls face. She cried out: 'You're hurting me — let me go!'

Roly forced her inexorably from the floor. She pulled away and stood glaring at him and rubbing her wrists.

'How dare you!'

'I'm sorry, Margy. I can't bear to see you that way. As though you're drunk or high on drugs. Your mother is worried. Come home.'

'Get lost!' she raged. 'I'll do as I like!'

Out of the dark loomed a young man. His hair was blond and spiky; his one earring small and neat. Muscled arms, heavily tattooed, bulged from a black vest.

'Leave my girl alone,' he growled and put an arm across Margy's shoulders. She moved closer to him. Roly started instinctively forwards. Margy put up her hands to ward him off.

'Go away, Roly. When I go home it

will be on Dirk's motorbike. I don't want you.'

Something very strange was happening to Roly. Suddenly his vaunted independence had lost its appeal. The sight of Margy — *his* Margy — snuggling up to an apparent yobbo was making it very difficult to keep his cool. He looked down at his hands. Unconsciously they had clenched into fists.

No-one was taking any notice. The heavy loud music beat on. The moving coloured lights made patterns over the sweating faces. He longed to feel his knuckles thump into Dirk's face and squelch that arrogant nose.

Dirk tightened his hold on Margy's shoulders and smirked triumphantly. Margy was watching him. What was she thinking? Was she hoping he would fight for her?

Roly sighed, unclenched his hands and slackened his shoulders. He didn't believe in violence. He was not afraid of Dirk but his better nature revolted at the thought of a fight. Just for a moment primitive instinct had taken over.

'Oh — get lost,' said Margy scornfully. Then she was back on the floor, hair tossing, hips gyrating. With a laugh Dirk followed her.

Roly was choked. How Margy would despise him! And who could blame her?

Going home a picture formed before his inner eye. Great splashes of orange and red, green and white. A picture without Margy. A picture of hell.

# 11

At the bottom of the hill the Rose Ann lay tidily in the loading bay. To Kate, troubled and unhappy, she looked a refuge. She remembered with nostalgia the days spent painting the woodwork and her easy, comradely relationship with Roly. That was what she needed now. Someone to talk to, someone to sympathise, someone who knew her well. Here, in Court Castle, she felt alien and unwanted.

She walked down the path, not hurrying, letting the faint breeze cool her cheeks and listening to a lark singing his bright song up and up into a pale blue sky. Soon he would be silent and plummet down. So, it seemed, it had been with her heart. Singing upwards and then falling into silence. Somehow she had to shake herself out of this foolishness.

She had been so happy and content with her wandering self-sufficient life. Learning her trade by practising it. She had not looked for any emotional entanglement. She had not wanted it. No way was it part of her plan.

The attraction she felt for Giles had stolen on her slowly and when she had thought he felt it too she had let herself become enmeshed. Now she must get herself in hand and learn again the freedom and felicities of those who walk alone.

There was no sign of Roly or Ailsa on the Rose Ann. The painted roses glowed softly in the afternoon sunshine and the boat lay silent.

'Roly!' Kate called, 'Are you there?'

The cabin door burst open and Roly emerged, dishevelled, unshaven, and very grumpy. Followed closely by Ailsa, clearly glad to be released into the fresh air, who bounded off the boat with friendly intent.

'Down Ailsa! Good girl! Roly — did you find Margy?'

'Yes,' said Roly, in a voice of deep gloom. 'I found her all right. Coming aboard?'

He stretched down a hand and helped Kate up.

'And is she coming home?'

'Don't know,' said Roly, sitting down heavily on a box. 'Silly female wouldn't talk sense. Got some dreadful ape of a biker in tow; couldn't get any communication going.'

Kate digested this.

'Is she trying to make you jealous?'

'Well, she did,' said Roly crossly. 'Didn't think she could do worse than a wastrel like me but now I'm not so sure. What a dive! And she looked dreadful. Mind you,' he said, after a pause for thought 'it could have been make-up. The things they do to their pretty faces these days baffles the mind.'

'You and I, Roly,' said Kate, 'are in the same boat in more ways than one. Let's have some coffee — strong.'

Soon they were both sitting with their

fingers laced round warm pottery mugs.

'And what's with you, Kate? Are you feeling trampled underfoot by these high-handed Harcourts?'

'It's Giles,' said Kate miserably, 'I let him get under my skin. He seemed so nice — and as if he really felt something for me.

'Usually I take very good care not to get involved with anyone while I'm on a job but this time . . . Well — it seemed different.'

Roly was looking at her speculatively. Despite the sadness in her eyes Kate, red curls glinting in the sun, cheeks flushing just a little from the steam heat of the coffee, was a charming sight. Roly, himself inoculated, could easily imagine the effect she would have on some other less wary male. And Giles, hard at work for so long building up a business from nothing, would be very vulnerable.

'So Giles fancies you, does he? I'm not surprised. What's in that to cast you down?'

'I *thought* he fancied me. But then that girl with the gold sports car turned up — Rowenda — and it was all kisses and 'darlings'. I'd forgotten about her. I suppose she's the girl friend. But then he shouldn't have made a pass at me.' She ended passionately: 'It isn't fair!'

'Don't be childish,' said Roly. 'You sound like Tamsin. I expect Giles thought you well able to take care of yourself. In any case that Rowenda is in a public relations firm — she's doing the brochure for the roses — they all go on like that.'

But Kate's heart had taken such a knock that she couldn't accept such an easy explanation.

'Are you telling me that she was never his girl friend?'

'Oh well. She's very attractive. She's been coming to Court Castle quite a lot. What would you expect? If he had any long term intention he never told me.'

Kate put down her empty coffee mug and looked around. The sun was going down the sky, flaming like fire in the many windows of the great house. She felt a lot better. Talking to Roly had helped, just as she had thought that it would. Ailsa was gazing at her looking expectant.

'I do like it here. Roly — could I stay the night? I need to get away — to think for a bit.'

'Why not?' said Roly. 'I can't lend you a toothbrush but the old trick of salt on your finger should do.'

They stood up and he put a brotherly arm around her shoulders. 'Come on, we'll walk Ailsa along to the Bargeman's Rest. It's a bit of a trudge from here but it will do you good. Then you'd better call Mary or she'll worry.'

\* \* \*

The 'phone rang at the house on the hill. Mary answered it.

'That was Kate,' she said, as she put the instrument back on its hook, 'she's staying the night with friends.'

Giles looked up from the papers he was reading, a frown between his eyes.

'What friends? I didn't know she had any friends in this area.'

'She must have,' objected Mary, 'she met lots of people when she was working on inn signs. Perhaps she's discussing new work. You know she's almost finished your grandmother's portrait again.' She looked thoughtfully at her son. 'We'll miss her, won't we?'

Giles grunted and returned to his reading. Mary smiled to herself.

★ ★ ★

Kate woke to the familiar feel of faint movement, the sound of water lightly slapping the quay heading and the bell-like call of a coot. She felt rested and relaxed and happy until she remembered why she was here. She banished the sinking feeling by scrambling out of the bunk and splashing her face with cold water.

There was no sign of Roly and Ailsa would be sleeping near him. Kate made herself a mug of tea and went into the forward cockpit. The sky was streaked with palest pink, the colour of a wild dog-rose. As Kate sniffed the dank scent of the canal she looked up towards the house behind which the sky was painted deeply with the flush of dawn.

Roly joined her, yawning hugely, and looking even more woolly and rumpled than usual. They had finished breakfast and Kate was in the galley doing the dishes when they were hailed from the bank.

'Ahoy, Rose Ann! Anyone awake?'

Kate stacked the last plate and emerged into the daylight. She found herself looking straight into a pair of hard blue eyes. Giles Harcourt stood on the bank. He wore a roll-necked blue sweater and his hands were in his pockets.

'Ah Kate,' he said coldly. 'Staying

with friends, I see?'

The sun had dispersed the wisps of coloured cloud and had risen above the rooftop. The light touched the man's smooth fair hair so that it gleamed like molten gold. He jerked his head impatiently to shift the straying lock which fell, as usual, across his forehead.

'Yes,' said Kate defiantly, 'not that its any business of yours.'

'Oh?' said Giles politely. 'I thought we were employing you?'

He jumped down into the boat which rocked as he landed. Kate glanced at him; every curl on her head, damped by her ablutions, seemed springy and tight with wrath.

'Not for much longer. Anyway, it's your mother I'm working for. I rang her yesterday as you evidently know. My *nights* are my own.'

'And Roly's, it seems,' said Giles smoothly.

Kate stared at him in astonishment.

'Don't be ridiculous!' But her voice faltered as she realised how it must look to him. 'What are you doing down here so early? Snooping?'

'This is my land and my boat,' said Giles wearily. 'I couldn't sleep. Came out for a walk.'

'Worrying about your roses, I suppose?'

'Yes. And other things. I don't feel like hassle. Goodbye to you.'

He turned and stepped up on to the bulwark as though to climb out of the boat. Roly was leaning against the cabin, grinning. Ailsa's head was poking out of the door. The knot of tension which had been tightening in Kate ever since she had seen Rowenda with her arms round Giles' neck, and heard the husky whisper 'darling' suddenly released like an over-wound spring. Without stopping to think she stepped forward holding both her hands out and pushed, outwards and sideways. Giles, caught off balance, toppled and fell. There was a tremendous splash and droplets of water were flung into the air to fall over Kate's hair, dampening it even further.

Ailsa barked, Roly roared with laughter, and Giles' head surfaced with hair plastered down and a spluttered swear word on its lips.

Kate froze with horror. How could she have been so silly? With the Rose Ann moored as she was, in the narrow creek, there was not that much clear water and Giles might well have struck his head on the stone quay as he went down. She found that she was shaking, goose pimples prickling the skin of her arms as if it was she, not Giles, who had been doused in canal water.

Giles reached up his hands and grasped the edge of the quay. With a tremendous heave he was out and sitting on the side. Roly was still chuckling.

'You want to watch out, Kate — you don't know your own strength!'

'I'm sorry,' said Kate, in a small voice. Her eyes were huge and imploring. 'I didn't mean — I shouldn't have . . .'

Giles swung his legs up and stood. He pushed the wet hair out of his eyes and shook himself.

'Is Margy home?' asked Roly.

Giles gave him a curious look.

'What's it to you?' he said. 'Yes — she's home. Turned up at 3 a.m. on the back of someone's motorbike. Slept in all yesterday. I've hardly seen her.'

'Good,' grunted Roly.

'I'll give her your regards,' said Giles sarcastically, and, squelching in his water-filled trainers, turned towards home. Kate started forwards.

'Giles,' she said beseechingly, 'I'm sorry — really I am.' But he didn't turn his head. Soon he broke into a loping run as he made his way back up the field path towards Court Castle.

Kate looked at Roly.

'Now I've done it,' she said, 'he'll never want to speak to me again.'

'Nonsense,' said Roly bracingly. 'Old Giles? Not the man to harbour a grudge.'

'Where's Kate?' asked Margy, when Giles came down to breakfast dried and changed and ready for work.

'Down on the Rose Ann,' said Giles unthinkingly, as he buttered a second slice of toast. The ducking had given him an appetite.

Margy said: 'With Roly?'

'Yes.'

'Why were you all wet when you came in?'

'Oh — I slipped and fell into the canal.'

'*You* did? Giles, I don't believe . . .'

'*I* did. We all have our off moments.'

Margy sipped her tea and looked thoughtful.

'Giles — was Kate there all night? She wasn't in her room when I looked earlier.'

'What of it?' said Giles. 'They're just *friends*.'

He said it very firmly, as much to convince himself as his sister. Margy banged her cup down on its saucer.

'I hate him,' she said fiercely. 'I'm not good enough for him but he has to act dog-in-the-manager and try and drag me away from having fun.'

She pushed back her chair and stormed out of the room. Giles sighed. Somehow he must put both Margy's problems and his own out of his mind. Rowenda and he had finished the copy for the brochure, so that was one thing out of the way, but there was a day of hard work to be done.

Kate came back to the house with her mind made up. She would leave as soon as possible. She was never going to find the serenity of her painted lady here. Her feelings were confused and her emotions in a turmoil.

While her delicate touch with a paintbrush had conjured up a tranquil beauty from the past she had been heavy-handed with her own personal relationships. The fact was that she had stayed too long at Court Castle, become too attached to the people living there.

It was high time she was back on the road again pursuing her own future in her own way.

She suddenly longed for the feel of the road beneath her feet, the weight of the pack on her back, even the ache of over-strained muscles which told her she had done well.

To sit on a grassy bank munching bread and cheese listening to the birds singing. To be her own woman, beholden to no man, choosing her own path. That was how it should be; that was right for her.

She came upon Margy, as she had the first time, casually dressed and weeding in the garden. There were dark smudges round the girl's eyes though whether these were caused by lack of sleep or the last remains of make-up it was hard to tell. She looked up at Kate resentfully.

'Giles told me,' she said. 'You spent the night with Roly. I thought you were my friend.'

'Don't be silly. I spent the night on

the Rose Ann as I have before. And not in Roly's bed if that is what you are implying.'

'So you say,' said Margy sulkily.

Kate looked at her in exasperation.

'What a family,' she said in disgust, 'minds like sewers. Anyway, you needn't worry, I'm going.'

'Going where? Back to the Rose Ann?'

'You're nuts. Back to the road. Away from all this muddle. Giles can have Rowenda and you can have Roly and I shall be free.'

'Rowenda?' said Margy, looking startled. 'Surely Giles wouldn't . . . I mean, she's nice enough in her way but not for *Giles*.'

'I don't know and I don't care,' said Kate, 'because I'm leaving and you can work it all out for yourselves.'

# 12

It was good to be back on the road. Kate kept to the lanes. The sun was hot and the banks were bright with the season's flowers; corn poppies, ox-eye daisies, and the small bright blue blossom of flax.

After a while she rested, took out her sketchbook and water-colour paints and recorded the delightful scene. She ate the sandwiches Mary had prepared for her lunch, climbed over the bank into a field and lay on the warm grass. A few whitish clouds drifted across the sky and Kate felt that she was drifting with them. Once again a skylark sang and sang, up and up, then suddenly was silent and fell. Yes — she had been right to leave Court Castle. Already her spirit was calmer; she didn't — she wouldn't — care about Giles; she let her thoughts go with the clouds.

★ ★ ★

Mary had been delighted with her copy of the portrait.

'It's just what I wanted — and it has a special charm of its own. The transparent pastel colours give the picture an ethereal quality the original doesn't have.

'I'm so glad you're pleased. I got very fond of the lady. I had to look at her so closely that I came to feel I knew her well.'

Mary said wistfully: 'I'm sorry you're going, Kate. You've been such a help and we shall all miss you. But I do understand that you have to get on with your life. Perhaps you'll come back and visit one day?'

'I'd like that,' said Kate politely, 'next summer perhaps? I hope to have a regular job by then but there'll be holidays . . .'

Privately she resolved that she would never come back. This strange interlude would be stored away in her mind, to be taken out and looked at sometimes, to be remembered as a beautiful dream.

Tidying up her workroom she was aware of a certain sadness. The oil painting in its ornate gold frame still leant against the oak chest-of-drawers. It was much too heavy for Kate to move. She took a last long look at the lady and at the rose, Empress Josephine, which lay across her hands. Then she covered the picture with a piece of old silk to protect it from the dust which danced, a thousand golden motes, in a beam of sunlight. The lady would have to wait until Giles came to move her.

Giles! Why did she have to think of him? Whatever feelings he might have had for Kate had surely been quenched by his undignified fall into the canal. And her own feelings were now in such chaos that all she longed for was to get away and regain peace and solitude. So Rowenda was only a business colleague; that was as maybe.

But it was certain that Kate had been gripped by unruly emotions which had caused her to lose her head and push her benefactor into some rather green and oily water.

He had not deserved it. All the time she had stayed at Court Castle Giles had been kind and helpful. It was all her wretched temper which flared up in these alarming little spurts when she was least expecting it.

The door opened and Giles was there. He took a step forward. Now he was dry; only his hair was a little more soft and floppy than usual from its extra wash. He was wearing the blue shirt that brought out the colour of his eyes. His face was pale and his expression set and rather stern. For a moment they stood there staring at each other.

Despite herself the image of Giles wet and furious came into Kate's mind and her lips began to curl upwards at the corners. Giles' face softened and his mouth too began to smile and all

171

of a sudden he broke into a great gust of laughter.

'Oh Kate — Kate — you little wretch! Why did you do it?'

'I saw you with Rowenda.'

'What? Oh! That's just the way these media people go on. You didn't think . . . '

'It's nothing to me,' said Kate stiffly, 'I only work here.'

He moved forwards and took her hands.

'Look at me, Kate. Is that all I am to you? An employer?'

'Not even that. It's your mother I work for.'

He was looking down at her with an expression of hope in his eyes.

'Don't go, Kate.'

She pulled her hands away.

'I must. Don't you see? It's all become a muddle.'

'No,' he said urgently. 'You've got in a muddle but I haven't. Stay with us, Kate. I . . . I . . . '

He wanted to say: 'I love you' but

her face was closed against him and he could not bear to put it to the test for fear she would rebuff him. But his face, which showed plainly the thoughts and feelings going on behind it, gave him away. He saw Kate flush a sudden fiery red. She stepped back.

'No, Giles, I've made up my mind,' she said. 'I'm glad you're not angry any more but I must be free.'

★ ★ ★

Now she stirred and sat up. The clear blue of the flax flowers was so like the colour of his eyes; but she had made her decision and must go on her way. Consulting a map, Kate found a route to a main road where she caught a bus. It was still sufficiently rural in this area for buses to pick up passengers between stops if they were flagged down. Kate was glad to sink back into a seat and watch the world go by outside the windows; her feet were aching.

It was late in the afternoon when she got off the bus. The town was small, so that one could glimpse the distant moors at the top of the steep hill up which Kate now trudged. Houses were old and picturesque and cobbled lanes led off the high street. Some of the shop fronts had bow windows and the architecture of the buildings was interesting and varied.

At the summit of the hill, to the left of the road, swept the great curtain wall of a castle. An archway, put there at some later date, opened out on to the street. Opposite this gateway was a teashop called — not surpringly — Castle Café.

Kate smiled ruefully to herself. There was no getting away from castles of one sort of another, it seemed; but she was tired and thirsty and needed somewhere to stay for the night. It was likely that local information as well as a cup of tea might lurk within. This shop, too, had a bow window. A bell tinkled as she opened the door and there was a step down. Inside the smell of freshly baked scones made Kate's mouth water.

A young woman stood behind a glass counter under which were arrayed plates of delicious-looking cakes and pastries. She had soft, pale gold hair fastened up at the back, partly hidden by a small white cap, and a sweet friendly face. Further on there was another step down and a bead curtain. Kate smiled at the girl.

'Can I get a cup of tea here?'

The great melting blue eyes under thick black lashes were welcoming. She gestured towards the interior.

'Of course. The dining-room is through there.'

Kate pushed aside the coloured lines of beads which clinked pleasantly behind her. The room was long with dark beams supporting a low ceiling. To the left latticed windows looked out on a small courtyard bright with bedding plants — geraniums in all shades from white through pink to scarlet, white and blue lobelia and golden pot marigolds. To the right was a hatchway with a counter and another door, evidently the way into the kitchen. But it was the end wall which held Kate's attention.

It was blank. There was nothing on it at all. Not a picture, not a shelf. Distempered cream-coloured, smooth and unsullied, it waited.

There was no-one else in the room. Kate chose a small table, the vase on which held a selection of garden flowers, and sat so that she could look at the wall.

The door into the kitchen opened and a man came out. He had brown hair, brown horn-rimmed spectacles, and a pleasant face. He wore a short white tunic with a mandarin collar which made him look a bit like a trendy hospital doctor. He carried a tray dangling from one hand and the words 'Castle Café' were embroidered in red thread across the left hand breast pocket. He walked over to Kate.

'What can I get you?' he enquired politely.

'A pot of tea, please and — are those fresh-baked scones I can smell?'

He nodded, looking pleased.

'Then I'll have some of those with strawberry jam,' decided Kate. 'Lots of them, please!'

He held up the tray with a pad against it while he noted her order, then deftly tidied the table, taking away redundant cutlery and plates to make more room.

When he had disappeared again into the kitchen Kate looked around with interest. Everything was neat and clean, polished and shining. The place had the air of somewhere that hadn't been open very long. It was strikingly fresh and pretty.

The tea was hot, strong and heartening, the scones and jam delicious. When she had eaten and drunk to repletion Kate leaned back in her chair to stare again at the empty wall. A picture began to form before her eyes; it dissolved away to be replaced by another. It was irresistible. She wondered, should she ask? Indeed she must!

She paid her bill to the young woman behind the counter.

'Could you tell me — are you the manageress?' (She didn't really think it likely but it seemed the most polite tack.)

The girl stared and then laughed.

'No, no,' she said, 'I just work here. It's Mr Robert you want. And he's the owner, not the manager.'

'Is he very busy?' asked Kate, 'or do you think I could speak to him for a moment?'

The girl glanced at the door into the street but since there didn't seem to be any more customers arriving at the moment she left her place and pushed apart the gaudy bead curtains.

'Mr Robert!' she called, 'there's a lady here wants to speak to you!'

The man who had served Kate her tea came into the front of the shop, an eager expression on his face. When

178

he saw Kate this changed to one of polite enquiry. Kate felt that all too ready blush creeping up on her again but took herself in hand.

'I'm Kate Trevine,' she said. 'I'm an artist and I'm touring the country working at anything that is needed.' She took a deep breath, for his face, though perfectly friendly, looked even more baffled.

'It's that wall,' she blurted out. 'That lovely plain wall at the end of your dining-room. It's just crying out to me to paint a picture on it!'

His face cleared and he laughed.

'What a very good idea,' he said, 'why didn't I think of that myself? Let's go and look at it.'

He held back the curtain so that Kate could precede him into the dining-room. They stood together and both surveyed the wall. Then Robert turned to Kate. She could almost see him thinking: 'Will she ruin my beautiful room with garish designs?'

Used to this reaction Kate took out

her sketch book and showed Robert the delicately transcribed flowers. There was professional ability here.

'These are good,' he said.

'I could use quick-drying paints,' said Kate eagerly. 'It needn't take all that long. What meals do you do?'

'At the moment I do a light lunch, just salads and things, and tea, of course. I haven't been open long.'

'So I could work in the mornings and perhaps early afternoons; and it would be easy to screen off during meals.'

'That would certainly be all right,' He looked thoughtful. 'Er — what do you charge?'

Kate laughed.

'Don't worry. If you'll feed me and buy the paints I only want a little pocket money to see me on my way to my next job when I move on. But there's one thing — I need somewhere to sleep. Do you live over the shop?'

'No, I don't.'

'Then perhaps you have an upstairs

room I could camp out in?'

He frowned.

'No. That won't do.'

'Oh,' Kate was downcast, 'then I'll have to ask for enough to put up somewhere and I expect that will make it all too expensive to be worth it. What a pity.'

She glanced wistfully at the tempting wall.

'You see I don't own the flat above. I just rent the ground floor. Then he brightened. 'But we needn't worry. I'm staying with my aunt just down the road while I get this place off the ground. She's got a spare room and I know she'd be pleased to have you. Wait a moment while I go and phone her.'

He was back in a few minutes looking triumphant.

'She'll be delighted. She's an amateur watercolourist herself and looks forward to meeting you. I'm Robert Preston, by the way.' He held out his hand. 'How do you do.'

His grip was strong and warm and the brown eyes behind the squarish frames were warm and friendly. The shop bell rang — and then again.

'Oh Lord,' said Robert, 'customers! I'm afraid I can't leave for a while yet. I'm doing everything myself except for selling at the counter. Daisy does that and cleans up before we open but I do all the rest. The ordering, the cooking and the serving.

'Will you mind waiting? You could go out and look round the town if you'd like.'

'I'd rather wait; said Kate. 'I've done enough looking for one day.'

'Good. Then you go back to your table and I'll bring you another cup of tea.'

He disappeared into the kitchen and came back with his tray and order book. Other customers were taking their places. Soon the room was full of the murmur of voices, laughter, and the chink of cups. Robert moved efficiently about carrying toast and cakes and jam and pots of tea. Delectable scents filled the air and Kate began to feel a little drowsy. Robert arrived at her table with a loaded tray that included chocolate eclairs with real cream.

'Goodness,' said Kate, eyeing these nervously, 'I shan't be able to eat again for a week. But I can't resist,' and she forked an eclair on to her plate and then bit into it, the cool fresh cream squishing into her mouth. Robert grinned and glided away.

The wall at the end of the room was a stage for her imagination. Should it be a picture of the town? The castle on the hill? Should she make it open out so that the eye was led on and up a path to the distant purple of the moors? Should it be a wood shading from spring to summer, then autumn to winter, so that the artist could introduce the many wild flowers that she loved and the creatures of the countryside — rabbits, squirrels, mice, a fox and badgers?

But the picture that persisted most

strongly, the one that took longest to fade, was a picture of the Rose Ann riding the waters of the canal with the elegantly drooping willow trees beyond.

# 13

Robert stood in the kitchen doorway watching Kate at work. His apprehensions had all gone. Dressed in paint-stained overalls, standing on a step-ladder, her red-gold curls tipped back and an expression of concentration on her face, she looked as Robert felt when he was creating something special for a meal.

The outline of the mural was almost complete: the distant moors, the bending willows, the gaily decorated narrow boat; and in the foreground grew golden kingcups, yellow flag iris, purple loosestrife and water forget-me-nots. A coot strutted, a mallard preened, a water vole prepared to 'plop'. It was a good day that had brought Kate Trevine into his café.

Kate and his aunt had taken to each other at once. Aunt Betty had bright black eyes, short iron grey hair and a beaky nose. She looked, Kate thought, like a kindly witch. In no time at all Kate was made free of his aunt's attic studio and shown the watercolour landscapes of the moors and town. There were several of the canal with the castle wall towering above.

'Oh!' exclaimed Kate, 'I didn't realise this town was on the canal. No wonder Mr Preston chose that design for the wall.'

Robert Preston had studied Kate's preliminary sketches carefully. He was attracted to the wood with its changing seasons but wanted something to do with the town. The moors, the castle, the old buildings; all these had charm. But quite a few tourists came from or to the canal and it was this picture that he finally chose, to Kate's delight.

She was very soon at home in Aunt Betty's little town house. The front door opened straight on to a steep cobbled street and from the back windows there was the distant view of the moors.

It was easy to be friends with Robert, a gentle, shy man, whose heart seemed to be entirely given to his café. Another, and much older aunt, from the other side of the family, had left him an unexpected legacy enabling him to stop working for other people and open his own business. Then Castle Café had come on the market, its owner emigrating, in a rather rundown condition. It was just what he wanted and he leased it at once.

Kate soon learned to use his first name and even managed sometimes, to coax him away from work to walk with her in the hills.

'For he's a workaholic, Kate,' said Aunt Betty. 'I'm very much afraid he'll make himself ill if he doesn't take a break from time to time.'

There was a cool breeze blowing across the heather and Kate's hands were stuffed deep in the pockets of her green anorak as they strode over the moors. Robert liked walking and led her upwards until they stood on a bracken edged ridge high above the town. Now they could see the whole of it: the grey and brown houses climbing the steep hills, the great circle of the castle wall with the smooth green centre dotted with later buildings, the silver strip of the canal with tiny boats floating on it; and further were fields and villages all made small by distance.

Robert sighed with pleasure. He stood with his hands resting on a sturdy ash plant, the breeze just lifting his hair. 'Look at it, Kate,' he said, 'isn't it like a dream? I've lived here all my life and wherever I go in the future I shall keep a home and my heart in this town.'

'It's lovely,' agreed Kate, 'but do you never want to wander away?'

She found this hard to believe. 'I want to create delicious and interesting food. I don't see any reason for doing it anywhere but here.' He paused, took off his glasses and ran the back of his hand across his eyes. He put them back and gazed into the distance. 'Only

Grace didn't understand. The world beckoned to her as it does to you. She said I'd come to nothing much mucking about in the kitchen in an out-of-the-way place like this.'

'I don't know who Grace was,' said Kate, 'but she was mistaken. There are plenty of ways you can make a name for yourself if you are really good. Then people will come to you from all over the country. Perhaps you'll write a book — appear on TV — become a household name. Was Grace your girl friend? Where is she now?'

'She went away,' said Robert simply. 'She said there was no future for us here.'

'I'm sorry,' said Kate, laying a hand comfortingly on his arm. He put his hand over hers for a moment and then took it away.

'Don't be,' he said. 'I suppose if I'd loved her enough I'd have given it all up. But I didn't — so it's probably for the best.'

Later Kate cautiously asked Aunt

Betty about the missing Grace.

Aunt Betty snorted.

'No loss, that one. Robert was always too good for her. What sort of a life did she think she'd have, wrenching a man away from his dreams? It won't do, my dear, as I expect you are bright enough to know.'

For a moment Kate's mind was full of roses.

But she had her own dreams. Only they were — less definite, less solid, still to be translated into reality.

Meanwhile life was very pleasant. The mural was taking shape and filling the shop with colour. Kate liked working with the scents of new baking and fresh ground coffee in the air. Robert would call her into the kitchen to admire his latest concoction and she began to fear that she would grow fat. Admiring so often meant tasting!

A technical problem which she had to solve was to make her painting fresh and bright and colourful and interesting and yet not allow it to dominate the room; not to let it push out and force itself on the diners. Just be there; so that when they looked up they were cheered and charmed and comforted.

Kate spent time exploring the town and looking at all the local features to which she was directed by Aunt Betty. Whenever she could, she dragged Robert out. Aunt Betty strongly approved: 'Just what he needs. A bit of fresh air and some intelligent company.'

Now the mural was nearly finished, Robert was beginning to realise how much he would miss her when she moved on.

Lying on the short grass on the edge of the moors, smelling the heather blossom and watching a pair of buzzards wheeling and mewing in the blue bowl of the sky, Robert stretched out an arm and pulled Kate down against his shoulder. She lay there for a moment, enjoying the comfortable feeling of protection; the rough fabric of the jacket he wore was pleasantly scented with cinnamon and spices.

He rubbed his cheek against her hair.

'Kate — Kate,' he murmured, 'it's been so lovely having you around. I wish . . . '

Kate twisted to a sitting position.

'Let's not spoil things, Robert,' she said. 'You know I've got to get another job. I've got to go.'

He looked up at her, brown eyes behind the heavy-rimmed glasses soft and gentle.

'Got to?'

'Yes. I'm not — I'm not *settled* in myself yet. I couldn't be like Aunt Betty. I couldn't be like Daisy and work in your shop. I'm really fond of you, Robert. Let's leave it at that.'

He laughed and sat up.

'And let's not be too serious on this splendid day! Race you down the hill!'

Panting, they arrived at the bottom of the slope. Kate laughed up at him.

'What you need, Robert, is to find yourself a local lass!'

* * *

As the mural neared completion the screen used to hide the paints was moved along and Kate worked on the finishing touches in full view of the customers. Sometimes tourists would leave their table to get a closer look, admire and exclaim and chat to Kate about her work.

One day Kate became aware that someone had been standing and staring for a longer time than usual but without saying a word. It began to make her feel slightly uneasy and at last she turned to see who it could be.

The man who stood there looked faintly familiar. But he showed no sign of recognising the artist so perhaps he was just a type. He wore a dark blue suit, a white shirt and a tie, quite unlike the gaudy outfits of most of the customers. Perhaps, Kate thought, he was a commercial traveller hoping to get an order from Robert. He returned her stare and smiled in what seemed to Kate to be a rather forced and formal manner.

'I hear you are a professional artist,' he said, 'earning a living by taking commissions as you travel around?'

'Yes, that's right,' said Kate, wondering what he was leading up to — was this the possibility of another job?

'Can you copy pictures?' was the next question.

'Indeed I can,' said Kate, 'that was my last job.'

'And you're really good?'

Kate looked baffled.

'See for yourself. I'm a qualified artist and picture restorer. I'm never short of work.'

His glance flickered over her and he seemed to make up his mind.

'I have a picture I want copied. Here is my card. If you are looking for work when you've finished here come and see me.'

'Thank you,' said Kate, a little stiffly. She didn't like his manner. As he turned away she stuck the little bit of card into the top pocket of her overalls. The man went back to his table and settled down with his pot of tea and a newspaper. Well — she didn't have to work for someone just because they asked. In this case she didn't intend to take up the offer.

Time passed pleasantly at Castle Café but soon it would be time for Kate to move on. Robert tried to think of some way of detaining her, but, apart from urging her not to work too hard there wasn't much he could do about it. He did think of asking her to paint a frieze in the shop section but most of the wall space was taken up by shelving and the huge mirror advertising a famous brand of tea in elegant old-fashioned gold lettering. Daisy went into fits of giggles when he consulted her and said that she didn't think it would be possible to squeeze in more than a thin line of ivy leaves.

'And that would make me feel crowded,' she pointed out.

Robert sighed. Daisy was quite right. So, instead, he urged Kate to go out on sketching expeditions with Aunt Betty. Here he met with unexpected resistance from the old lady.

'Don't be absurd, Robert. I've got plenty to do around the house and, in any case, sketching is not something I do with another person. Part of the charm is being alone with one's thoughts. Kate doesn't want me.'

In fact Kate would have been happy to have her company but Aunt Betty was adamant. So Kate wandered around the town by herself. Soon she would have to go — soon — but not quite yet.

On the other side of the castle from the street with the café the mound sloped, green and smooth, down to the canal. Halfway up was a wooden bench which commanded a splendid view of the water and the boats and the distant willow strewn wetlands. This was one of Kate's favourite spots.

On a sunny afternoon, drowsing in the heat of late summer, she sat there watching the sunlight on the water and listening to the swifts screaming as they swooped above the ancient stones. Her drawing block lay on her lap and a pencil dangled idly from her fingers.

She was scarcely thinking — just absorbing the colour and warmth and scents of summer.

Down below several canal boats were tied up along the bank. This was the place where tourists landed to view the historic old town. Another boat chugged its way slowly into sight. Kate noted with appreciation that this was an old one. Some of those moored below had been built especially for the tourist trade.

This was a handsome converted narrow boat; bright with fresh paint and the traditional floral ornamentation.

But it was not, thought Kate critically, as beautiful as the Rose Ann. It came in directly below where Kate was sitting. The voices, floating up through the clear air, were American. It seemed to have been hired by an American family party.

They crowded into the cockpit talking and laughing and pointing up the hill. There seemed to be a middle-aged couple, a boy, and two teenage girls. It made sense as a way of seeing England; moving slowly, absorbing the atmosphere. A much better plan than motoring from place to place with all the noise and hassle that this entails.

Kate watched idly as one of the girls stepped off the boat. The others did not follow but called farewells and waved in a friendly manner. One of the passengers seemed to be leaving the party and going on their own way.

The narrow winding path led up the hill and passed quite close to the bench on which Kate was sitting. She sat up suddenly, jolted by surprise.

The girl was wearing white shorts and a sweatshirt of a particularly striking turquoise. As she stopped waving to her friends and turned her head, smooth toffee-coloured hair bouncing, she looked up and her grey eyes widened with astonishment.

'Kate!' she cried and came bounding up the path.

It was Tamsin.

# 14

'Whatever are you doing here on your own?'

Kate was horrified.

Tamsin was looking very pleased with herself.

'Same as you!' she retorted, and joined Kate on the bench.

'I have work here.' Tamsin was looking at Kate's sketch.

'That's good,' she said approvingly.

'Don't change the subject!'

'Don't fuss, Kate,' Tamsin begged. 'I left a note to say not to worry. That I had some money and I'd be back.'

'Not to worry!'

Kate could imagine.

'I couldn't just stay around there. Giles is gloomy, Margy is always out, and Mike wouldn't take me to the disco.'

'What were you doing on that boat?' Kate pointed. The American party had disappeared inside.

'I took a bus and got off in a village with a nice name — Winleaton, I think it was. I was sitting by the canal wondering what to do next when I heard American voices. Gee — that was homey! So I went and made friends and they gave me a lift here in the Gold Belle because they said this town had the biggest and best castle for miles around. And they sure were right. It's great, isn't it?'

'It's a fine castle,' agreed Kate. 'But when was this, Tamsin? We're a fair way from Court Castle here.'

'Only yesterday,' said Tamsin. 'I got up very early and left before breakfast.'

'Yesterday! Then you've been away all night?'

'Sure have,' said Tamsin happily, 'they had a spare bunk on the boat and I was really useful.'

'I expect you were,' said Kate helplessly. She didn't know whether to giggle or burst into tears. The whole thing was preposterous. Mary would be demented with worry and Giles would be furious.

'I worked the locks,' said Tamsin proudly. 'And they said I learned to do it right quick. But I'm sure glad to find you, Kate. I expect you'll know where I can get a meal and a bed for the night?'

Kate thought rapidly. Yes, she could rely on Aunt Betty to take in the American waif without making a big to — do about it.

'Are you hungry?' she asked.

'I'm always hungry,' said Tamsin simply.

'Didn't they feed you enough on the Gold Belle?'

'Sure did. But food doesn't last you long at my age,' explained Tamsin.

'Come on,' said Kate. She put away her sketching things and stood up. 'I'm going to take you to the café where I'm working and feed you.'

'Why are you working in a café?'

Tamsin stood too and followed Kate up the slope.

'I'm painting a mural on a wall.'

'Sounds fun,' said Tamsin enviously.

'It has been fun but I've nearly finished. And another thing, Tamsin, I'm going to telephone the Harcourts at once and tell them where you are.'

Tamsin stopped.

'Kate! Don't be such a spoil-sport! I want to see this really old castle and I'd much rather be with you than with that lot. They're all boring. At least,' she added, 'they are being boring just now.'

'Hurry up,' said Kate. 'I thought you said you were hungry? I *must* ring the Harcourts. They'll be worried sick. Haven't you any consideration for others, you wretched child?'

'I don't see why they should care,' grumbled Tamsin, but she followed Kate round the other side of the wall and down towards the street.

'They care because they are responsible for you. Your grandparents trusted them to look after you. And they are fond of you, Tamsin. They'll be imagining you cold and hungry and all sorts of things.'

'Well, I am hungry,' said Tamsin.

Soon she was seated at one of the small café tables tucking into a plate of baked beans on toast and drinking a large glass of coke. Kate explained to Robert who was very amused but too busy to give much attention except to tell Kate to feel free to succour her protegeé any way she wished.

Mary answered the phone.

'Kate? What? You have *Tamsin* with you? Oh, thank God. We've been wondering whether to call the police and hoping she would ring or come home. They are so *thoughtless* at that age. She's quite all right? Where are you?'

Then Giles came on the line. He sounded tired and cross.

'I'm coming over to fetch her at once,' he snapped.

'No — no Giles, wait. I've promised

Tamsin she can see over the castle now that she's here. Come tomorrow. She's perfectly all right, I assure you.'

Tamsin had finished her meal and was admiring Kate's mural. 'It's lovely. So real. I could almost step on to that boat.'

'Thank you. Now listen — I've just spoken to Giles. He wants to fetch you home at once.'

'Oh, no!'

Dismayed, Tamsin spun round.

'No. I asked him to come tomorrow. After making such an exciting journey I thought you ought to be allowed time to see things. But mind — no running off again!'

'No, I won't,' promised Tamsin. 'I expect I'd get pretty hungry without three regular meals a day — and snacks!'

Aunt Betty took to Tamsin at once and gave her a large glass of milk and a slice of home-made plum cake 'just to fill any gaps until the next meal.'

She sat down by the child's side in

the small cosy parlour and plied her with questions about America.

'It's always been a dream of mine,' she sighed, 'to visit the United States. But I don't know anyone there and hotels are so lonely.'

'You know someone now,' said Tamsin. 'You shall be my aunt too and when I go home to college you can come and stay.'

Aunt Betty laughed very hard.

'That's truly nice of you! I'll remember!'

'And so shall I,' said Tamsin firmly.

Aunt Betty took Tamsin off to show her sketches of the castle. Tamsin admired them sincerely.

'I think that's what I'll do,' she said. 'I'll learn to paint. Then I'll always have an interesting occupation. I wish you were still at Court Castle, Kate. Then you could teach me.'

'Just get some paints and have a go,' advised Kate.

In the morning Kate and Tamsin visited the castle. The centre of the site, inside the wall, was dotted with fortifications. It was possible to climb the narrow winding stairs, pausing to peer through arrow slits, in one or two turrets; to come out on top and look out over battlements to the water meadows on one side and the tumbled roofs of the town on the other. Tamsin felt she was really in touch with English history and squealed with delight as she clambered and clung.

Afterwards Kate took her down one of the steep cobbled streets to a bow-windowed shop where she helped to choose a box of watercolour paints, brushes, pencils and a sketch pad. Greatly satisfied, Tamsin stowed these treasures away in a canvas satchel provided by Aunt Betty.

When Giles walked into the café dining room he saw Kate standing in front of her mural explaining the various features to Tamsin.

'I didn't make up the flowers,' she was saying, 'they really are flowers you might find by the canal and I have tried to make them accurate.'

'You are clever, Kate,' said Tamsin. 'I wonder if I shall ever be able to do anything like that?'

'Of course you will,' said Kate, 'if that is what you want to do. But everyone has a different style and wants to create different things. Take Roly, for instance. He likes great swathes of colour. Not something I could do at all.'

'I didn't know Roly was a painter.'

'We were at art college together. He used to be very good indeed.'

It was the afternoon pause between lunch and tea. There was no-one in the room except the two girls absorbed in looking at the mural. Beyond the window the tiny courtyard garden glowed in the afternoon sun. He saw the two heads, one smooth and shiny as sucked caramel, the other a mass of tight copper curls. Sensing they were being watched they turned together.

Tamsin's face registered a struggle between pleasure at seeing Giles and chagrin at having to go. Pleasure won and she ran forwards.

'You tiresome brat,' said Giles amiably, giving her a brotherly hug, 'I don't know why I bother with you. I should be delighted when you run away.'

'You like me, Giles, that's why,' said Tamsin smugly.

'Perhaps.' Giles looked over her head. 'Pleased to see me, Kate?' he queried, raising one eyebrow.

Kate said nothing but 'hallo' hoping that he could not read in her face just how pleased she was. This was the man she had tried to forget, the man who nevertheless found his way into her thoughts and into her dreams. She didn't want to become involved, to be vulnerable to someone else's wayward impulses. She meant to concentrate on her work and keep away from personal relationships. But seeing him standing there, tall and strong and kind, with that uncontrollable lock of fair hair flopping over his forehead, brought vividly back to her the feel of his lips on hers. She longed to stroke back that straying lock; to be where Tamsin was, close and protected.

He put Tamsin gently aside and came across the room.

'So this is the current project.' He walked the length of the wall and returned. 'It's splendid. It really is. Not just the realistic detail, the whole feel of the piece. One can almost hear the water lapping against the sides of the boat. One day you must paint a picture of the Rose Ann for me.'

At the moment Robert came out of the kitchen. Kate introduced the two men who shook hands.

'I think you are to be congratulated on having Kate to do your wall picture. She's going to be famous one day. People will come here just to see it.'

'I agree,' said Robert, 'but I hope they will also come to sample my cooking.'

'Robert will be famous long before I

am,' said Kate, smiling at him.

'Thanks, Kate!' he turned to Giles. 'I do hope you will take tea here before you go?'

'Oh yes, let's,' said Tamsin eagerly. 'Such sumptuous cakes, Giles! Can we — please?'

Soon they were seated near the window eating buttered crumpets and drinking Earl Grey tea while a plate piled high with cream cakes stood offering temptation in the middle of the table. Tamsin's mouth was too full to allow speech but Kate asked: 'How is every thing at your home? I hope your mother wasn't too upset when Tamsin took off like that.'

'I'm afraid she was, rather,' said Giles. 'But of course she's all right now and looking forward to having the child back.'

'It seems Tamsin was bored,'

'I know and I'm sorry. But it's more difficult than we realised to entertain such a young lady. We all have work to do. And Margy, who is nearest her age, is away an awful lot.'

'Tamsin says Mike won't take her to the disco.'

Giles said: 'I'm very glad to hear it. He has a lot of sense, young Mike.'

'I don't see why that's sensible,' grumbled Tamsin through a mouthful of cream. 'I think it's stupid.'

'When Margy is at home she does the garden and looks after the goat and Tamsin helps; but she's been away so often that I've had to take on an extra hand to keep the formal gardens tidy. They are a showcase for the business and the fount of the whole thing. This chap came to the door one day looking for a job. A small fellow but quite handy.'

'I think Tamsin will find more to do from now on. She's decided to be an artist, too, haven't you Tamsin?'

'Yes. And Giles, Kate bought me paints and everything and Aunt Betty found me a satchel and Kate says to just do it and learn as I go.'

'That's a good idea,' said Giles, much struck by the thought of his obstreperous charge sitting quietly painting.

'But I wish Kate was coming too,' said Tamsin. 'It was much more fun when Kate was there.'

'Yes. It was, wasn't it?' said Giles. 'I wish you would come back, Kate.'

'I told you. I finished the job,' said Kate stubbornly.

'But I have another job for you,' said Giles.

She looked at him doubtfully.

'A real job?'

'A very real job. And important to me.'

'What is that?'

'We were talking over the brochure, Rowenda and I, when she said that what I needed was really original art work. Not just the colour photographs that most people use. She said what a pity you'd gone as you could have done beautiful watercolours instead.'

'*Rowenda* said that?'

'Rowenda is an excellent business

woman. You have the wrong idea about her, Kate.'

Kate doubted it, remembering how Rowenda had looked at Giles. But it certainly was interesting that the other girl had come up with this idea. It showed that Rowenda, too, treated her work as of supreme importance.

At once, in her mind, she began to visualise the roses on the page.

'Isn't it late now, for roses?'

'There can be roses up to Christmas if the weather is kind. And I have so many varieties that there'll be beauties in bloom right now. Of course it won't be for this year. That catalogue will be going out soon for people to buy bareroot plants in the winter to plant from November to March. But a start could be made for next year.'

Tamsin was looking eager.

'Do come, Kate. Then you can teach me. I know you say I can just do it but I'm sure I'd get on a lot faster with help.'

'Yes. Do come, Kate,' said Giles.

Kate hesitated. It was a lovely idea. Flower painting was the thing closest to her heart. But if she went back — had she the strength of mind to stay emotionally uninvolved? She'd been at Court Castle too long already.

She looked across at Giles. His eyes were on hers and they were almost beseeching. How could she see her way clearly when she was swamped by primitive feelings? She felt a weakening of her resolve and braced herself. This job he was offering — it was open ended. If she returned to paint roses she would certainly still be there by the following June. What then of her plan to try this and that, to roam the land, to please only herself?

If she went back to Court Castle she would get more and more tangled in the lives of these people and would never break free again.

She looked back at Giles. With an effort she said: 'I'm sorry. I can't.'

'Why not? Have you another job?'

He did not believe her.

All at once Kate remembered the man who had given her a card with his address and the offer of work.

'Yes,' she said firmly. 'I have.'

# 15

'So that was your last employer,' said Robert. 'I can see now why you can't get interested in an ordinary bloke like me.'

Kate blushed furiously.

'Don't be ridiculous. Anyway, you're not an ordinary bloke, remember? You're this charismatic café proprietor who is going to make a big hit on TV!'

Robert laughed.

'So you say! Are you really leaving, Kate?'

'Yes. I must get on. I've quite finished the mural.'

'And very splendid it is too,' said Robert with approval. 'It was a lucky day for me when you walked into my shop.'

Kate looked at her picture transforming the wall, colours glowing. But her eyes were strangely misty and, though she blinked rapidly, did not clear.

She was seeing Giles' face when she refused his offer. He'd known just how much she must have longed to take the commission and how strong, therefore, must be her resolution not to return. He had taken her hand in farewell and made some commonplace remark in a cool voice but his eyes were sad.

Tamsin threw her arms round Kate's neck.

'I wish you'd come, Kate. It will be so dull without you.'

Kate hugged her back.

'You'll be all right.'

Her voice was a little husky.

'That's that, then,' said Giles.

The old car had gone clattering off down the cobbles leaving emptiness behind it.

Now it was once more time to go forth into the unknown.

Kate shouldered her pack and set off up into the hills. There was no hurry.

Her pack contained a splendid picnic put up by Aunt Betty including some delicious examples of Robert's cooking. The address on the card was some way over the moors but Kate was glad to stretch her legs and be out on the road again. The air was sweet with heather and gorse. Sheep wandered on the road. There were few cars.

She told herself fiercely that this was all she wanted from life. Another job to go to; a new place to see. She would not become so fond of any man again that he had power to destroy her. She remembered how, at art college, after Roly had gone, she had lost the will to work. Everything was dust and ashes. Her drawing was mechanical. All the fire and originality went out of her painting. The delicate flower portraits, at which she had excelled, became conventional and standardised.

One day her tutor called her to his study. He had before him a pile of her sketches which he turned over, a frown between his brows.

'What's the matter, Kate? Where's it all gone? You were one of my best students.'

Kate felt the warm colour rush up her neck to redden cheeks and then forehead. She said nothing, just looked at him with large anguished eyes.

Bill Janis said impatiently: 'Man trouble, I suppose. You've got to learn, if you are going to achieve anything, not to let your heart ruin you hand. It does not have to be like that. A real artist — and you could be a real artist — takes the dark side of life and makes it work. Makes it work — that's what matters. Remember that, Kate.'

And she had remembered. She had concentrated on work until one day she realised that she had worked Roly out of her system. No way would she risk going back to that desolate place again.

Very nearly she had forgotten; very nearly she had become vulnerable once more. But she had made a decision and broken away. Now she was her own woman — but she did not feel the sense of elation that she ought.

Kate stayed that night in a small pub in a moorland village. After all that tramping she slept well. In the morning she discovered that the local bus was making one of its biweekly calls and could take her where she wished to go.

The bus set her down in a huddle of stone houses that was nothing more than a hamlet. An elderly man sat on a bench by the bus stop, an old black and white collie at his feet.

'Excuse me,' said Kate, 'can you tell me which way I go for Moor End Farm?'

The man pushed his cap on to the back of his head and stared up at her.

'Moor End Farm, lass? That's a tidy way on. Take the first left down road and then left again. You'll not miss it.' He chuckled. 'It's only house down that way, do you see!'

221

Something made Kate ask: 'When does the bus return?'

'Ten of the morning tomorrow. That's market day, do you see.'

'Thank you,' she said, and turned to walk away.

'I'll be on it myself,' said her informant. 'I'll look out for you.'

'Oh — I don't know if I'll be back by then.'

'You'll be back. If you're going to Moor End Farm, you'll be back.'

Kate smiled and waved and went on her way, wondering what her new acquaintance meant. It was true that Mr Stringer hadn't had a very attractive persona but he'd seemed a reasonably businesslike type and had assured her that she would not be the only woman in the house.

The road to the left bore down the hill. After a while it branched again and became a rough track, stony and rutted. A few stunted thorn bushes grew at the sides. The road dipped and in a hollow Kate could see the house.

It was substantial, three stories high, made of granite blocks and very old. At the back stood a cluster of farm buildings. There was no garden to the front, just a path of sunken slabs leading to the front door. It looked deserted, slightly neglected, and rather uninviting.

Kate told herself not to be silly and walked firmly up the path. There was an electric bell. She held her finger on it for a moment and heard it ringing somewhere distant down a passage.

Footsteps approached. The door opened. The woman standing there was very tall, very beautiful, with fair hair plaited in a coronet and a cold, unfriendly face.

'Yes?' she said.

'I'm Kate Trevine. Mr Stringer asked me to call to see about working on some pictures.'

The woman looked her over dismissively.

'You? You know about oil paintings?' She did not move back.

'Yes,' said Kate, feeling the ready flush of rising temper. 'I am an artist.'

A man's voice called down the passage.

'Helen! Let Miss Trevine in at once!'

The woman stood aside and Kate stepped into the house. The hallway was very high and rather dark, lit by one low-powered bulb. It smelt a little damp; not quite clean. The patterned carpet was worn through to the warp in places. Mr Stringer came out of a back room and moved forwards with hand outstretched.

'Miss Trevine. So glad you could come. Helen — Miss Trevine would like a cup of tea, I'm sure. Come in; come in.'

Kate was glad of the tea and John Stringer engaged her in amiable chat about her work and the places she had visited. He seemed particularly interested in Court Castle. Presently he led her further along the passage and into a room where a large oil painting stood propped against the wall. He walked over and turned the frame so that Kate could see by the light through a window.

It was a group portrait — a man, a woman, two children and a dog. The figures were in old-fashioned dress and posed against a green hill with a ruined temple in the far distance and a clump of formal trees mid-distance to the right. The picture was in oils and the colours deep and rich. Kate looked at it with great interest. It seemed familiar — had she seen it before?

'Is it valuable?' she asked.

John Stringer shrugged.

'Who can say? Perhaps. For the moment the problem is that it is badly damaged. Can you fix it?'

Across one corner of the picture were six deep scratches. They ran over blue sky and white cloud and green grass but not across the figures. Nor was the canvas torn although the thick paint was deeply scored. Kate touched the marks gently with her finger-tips.

'What a shame,' she said. 'Yes. I

225

can help. I'll be glad to. But I'll need special materials. I'll have to take a trip into the nearest town.'

Mr Stringer tenderly covered the canvas with a cloth and then turned it back against the wall.

'No need for you to go,' he said. 'Make out a list and I'll fetch what you want in the morning.'

'But I prefer to choose my own . . .'

'No need,' he repeated abruptly, with an air of finality.

'Oh!'

Kate was going to argue but there was something about the set of his shoulders as he led the way out of the room that made it seem not worth the effort. She shrugged — it didn't matter that much — and followed without further comment.

The bedroom to which she was shown was comfortable enough. It would do. She couldn't expect the homey comfort of Aunt Betty's little house or the comparative luxury of Court Castle on every job. At least the work was going to be interesting and well worth doing. She wondered how the picture had come to be damaged and what it was doing at this lonely, rather rundown, house in the moors. Perhaps Mr Stringer had inherited it all recently and was now trying to get things in order. Yes. That made some kind of sense.

Tired from her travels, Kate woke late next morning. The sun was quite high already, filling the hollow in the hills with light. Finding the house gloomy, Kate took her mug of coffee and sat on a wooden bench outside the kitchen door. Presently Helen Stringer followed her.

'Is Mr Stringer about?' asked Kate.

'No. He took the car and your list of materials and went off some time ago. He'll not be back yet awhile.'

Kate sipped her coffee and looked up at the blue bowl of the sky. Helen looked at Kate. It was bad enough being stuck in this dismal house while John nursed his obsession without having him bring in a beautiful redhead and expect her to look after the girl. Kate's glowing curls, creamy freckle-dusted skin, and clear green eyes made the older woman feel tired and crumpled. It was no good telling herself that John wasn't like that — all he cared about were his beastly pictures. No man, thought Helen, could be totally impervious to such fresh beauty.

'When you've finished your coffee I'll show you something interesting,' Helen offered. 'Something I think you ought to see before you make up your mind to take this job.'

Kate looked surprised.

'I thought I *had* made up my mind.'

Helen smiled a touch grimly.

'Perhaps. But come and see.'

This time Kate was led upstairs, past the floor on which she had slept, and up again to the top of the house. It was drier up here, but there was no carpet on the floor, there were no curtains at the windows. Helen threw open the door of a large room and stood aside.

'There,' she said, 'that is what John has brought you here to do. The one you saw yesterday is the easiest, I should think.'

Kate saw a room full of oil paintings. Hung on walls, stacked against walls, lying on tables, or simply piled one on top of another on the floor. Many, she could see even from the doorway, were marked or damaged in some way. The effect was extraordinary. Like some hospital waiting-room with the patients huddled and expectant.

'Goodness!' she gasped, 'he doesn't mean me to work on all those?'

'Oh yes he does. And he'll see you stay until you've done the lot.'

'See I stay? How can he?'

'Oh — he can all right. We have no 'phone. We're away from the road. And John has a persuasive tongue. He'll offer you lots of money. He'll make you feel it's your duty. You'll stay.'

Kate was staring in amazement at the pile of canvases.

'Where did he get them all? Why are so many damaged?'

'Oh — he collects. Goes to country auctions — that kind of thing. You get lots cheap if they are not perfect.'

Kate had moved into the room and was looking more closely. Some of the pictures were very old and very beautiful, painted with power and vision. She had the uncanny feeling that she was looking at the children of great artists. That they were crying out to her: 'Kate — Kate — we need you. Look after us!'

Helen leant against the doorway, watching. Her expression was cynical.

'No — it wouldn't be hard for John to persuade you to stay. And once you got embroiled in his plans you'd never get away.'

Kate forced herself back to the door. The whole atmosphere of the house was claustrophobic and strange.

'You're right. I'm glad you showed me. I must go now, before Mr Stringer returns.

Kate packed swiftly and Helen saw her to the door. Kate hesitated before leaving.

'Thank you,' she said. 'What will you tell Mr Stringer?'

'That you changed your mind,' said the other woman. 'What can he do about that? Hurry now — you'll just catch the bus.'

Helen Stringer watched as Kate disappeared over the top of the hill. John would be very angry but he'd get over it and Helen's heart was the lighter as such obvious temptation was removed.

Kate's elderly friend was just boarding the bus, without the collie dog, when she arrived. Thankfully she climbed on and paid her fare. The bus chugged determinedly up and down the hills and valleys. The man leant across the aisle to speak to Kate.

'Knew you'd be here,' he said. 'Not a place to stay, Moor End Farm.'

'No,' agreed Kate, 'but why not?'

'Funny goings-on, do you see. Cars

and things in the middle of the night. Never anything in the daylight like honest folk. Don't know why she stays with him, sour crab that he is.'

Kate giggled. It made her feel a lot better sitting here in the sunlight listening to gossip while the Stringers and their dismal house got further and further away.

'You can't win them all,' she thought philosophically. Now she was retracing her steps. Not a part of her plan. Odd how light-hearted she felt.

Kate stepped down into the shop. It was the same — why shouldn't it be? Yet it seemed a long, long while since she had left, so strange and so disturbing had been the interlude.

There was the gilt lettered mirror, shelves stacked with new loaves, the glass counter covering plates of delectable cakes and scones. The atmosphere was warm and pleasantly scented with spice and the fresh baked bread.

Kate parted the bead curtains and went through the door into the kitchen where the delicious smells hung even thicker in the air.

'Robert?' she queried, then stopped and stared. Before her two figures merged together. Robert's arms were round Daisy whose white cap had slipped from her head releasing a tumble of golden locks. Robert's head was bent over hers and he was busy kissing willing lips. He raised his head and blinked at Kate then fumbled for his spectacles with one hand, the other keeping a firm grip on his charming prisoner. Managing to perch the glasses back on his nose his vision cleared and he smiled a happy welcome.

'Kate! What brings you back this way so soon? You're the first to hear our news. Daisy and I are going to be married!'

Daisy raised a pink and bashful face and tried to smooth back her rumpled hair. The big blue eyes were pools of happiness.

'Hallo!' she whispered.

'I'm so glad for you both,' said Kate.

'It couldn't be better. You make a perfect couple.'

'Yes,' said Robert fondly, looking down at his willing captive, 'I'm a very lucky man.'

The look that Daisy cast up at him from under the thick black lashes was one of such adoration that, visitor or no visitor, Robert kissed her again.

Kate began to back off. Robert looked up, grinning.

'Sorry,' he said. 'I just can't believe my luck! Don't go, Kate. Stay and have a celebratory meal with us and tell us all your news.'

Kate shook her head.

'Oh no,' she said. 'I can see you've got better things to do! I'll drop in on Aunt Betty and tell it all to her.'

Aunt Betty was delighted to see Kate and listened with alert interest to the tale Kate had to tell. Then she nodded.

'Sounds like a scoundrel to me,' she said. 'Country auctions? he'd be so lucky. You were right to take that lady's advice and get out of it. What will you do now?'

'I don't know,' confessed Kate. 'I haven't got another definite job to go to. That's unusual — but then I've never before given up on one. Something will turn up; it always does.'

'Didn't Giles Harcourt offer you another job?'

'Yes,' said Kate uneasily, 'but it would be a very long term project and put a stop to my summer-time wandering.'

'Winter will put a stop to that in good time in any case. What then? Home to your parents and a nice safe job in an advertising agency?'

'It's not winter yet,' said Kate. 'I've got a bit more wandering to do.'

But she wondered, as she shouldered her pack and set off again, why the thought of new work in new places no longer held the same appeal. Was she bored already? Somehow she didn't want to keep roaming. Somehow her steps turned backwards along paths already trodden. Of course she rationalised it. She was more likely to get work where a sample of her skills was already displayed and admired.

Here was the White Swan. There hung her sign, the swan proudly wearing his golden coronet as he sailed on a pool of azure blue. But now benches and tables were set in the pub garden and they were crowded with people and stacked with pint pots. Families picnicked and children and dogs tumbled and screamed over the short grass.

Kate went inside. It was dark and cool after the bright sunshine. Vera presided; very busy, very smart. She greeted Kate with pleasure and called up the attention of one or two regulars.

'Kate — who painted our sign — you remember?'

But she could not pause long from serving drinks and snacks to eager customers. Kate was glad to see the White Swan doing such good business. She ordered a glass of cider and a cheese roll and took them outside. It was nice but not the same. Time had passed, things had changed, and now that she had no part in it, contributed nothing, she felt what she was — a stranger.

The grass was dry and the sun warm and, as she munched her bun and sipped her cider, Kate felt her problems dissolve. She gazed up at the sign, bright and gleaming in the sun, and found it quite hard to believe it was all her own work. Then one of the lads she remembered picked up his pint and came over to her. He was a nice boy, thin and gangly with ears that stuck out but an engaging smile.

'Hallo, Kate. Admiring your work? It's great!'

'Thanks, Fred. It is rather jolly, isn't it?'

'I'll say.'

He collapsed his lanky legs and subsided on to the grass next to her.

'Kate — I was wondering . . . '

'Yes?'

'I was wondering if you'd do a job for me?'

Kate stared at him.

'You?'

'Yeah. Well — our group. We play all around at dances and parties and things.'

'Whatever could I do for you?'

'It's like this. We've got an old van. And I thought — Kate could make that look real grand. With our name on it and lots of bright colours. You could — couldn't you Kate? What do you say?'

He looked at her eagerly.

'Why not?' said Kate. 'I've nothing on at the moment.'

Fred took another swig of his pint and wiped the back of his hand across his mouth.

'Only thing is — do you charge an awful lot? We haven't been going long and don't raise much more then expenses.'

Funny how life went. First Mr Stringer and his dubious loot and now this, but her heart lifted.

'Don't worry, Fred. For you — somewhere to sleep, three meals a day, and the price of the paints. I shall enjoy it. I've never done a van before!'

Fred's face lit up.

'You're a grand lass. That'll be no problem. Me Ma'll look after you.'

Vera came out of the pub and stood in the doorway. The drinking crowd had thinned. Fred stood up and waved.

'Here — Vera! Come and tell Kate that me Ma's all right!'

Vera came over.

'Oh, aye. Fred's Ma'll see you right. But what a turn-up for the books. Kate Trevine and a psychedelic van!'

'I'll try my hand at anything once. What's the name of your group, Fred?'

He grinned sheepishly.

'We call ourselves Canal Creatures.'

'Uh! What a picture!'

Kate's mind became full of monsters poking up horned heads from water symbolised by green and purple streaks. She began to laugh.

'This is going to be fun!'

The van in its current state was battered and shabby. The group had a card with their title scrawled on it which they hung on the handles of the back doors when they went off performing and that was all. The outfit could certainly do with a face lift.

Fred's mother lived in a small farmhouse on the outskirts of the village. Fred asked Kate to wait outside while he went indoors to explain about her unpaying guest. Hens free-ranged round the yard pecking amongst straws and pebbles. There were various outbuildings and a glimpse of cows in a field over a five-barred gate. A horse poked its head over a stable door. A working farm. A line of sheets flapped in the breeze on a washing line in the orchard. It did not look like the kind of place where an uninvited extra would be welcome. Uninvited, at any rate, by the lady of the house.

The door opened. A large woman stood there, her hands on her hips, a flowered apron tied round an ample waist.

'Ho,' she said fiercely, 'so you're the one. I might have known it. Artist indeed! One of these camp followers more likely!'

Kate resisted the temptation to laugh. Fred's face, eyes popping, appeared over his mother's shoulder. He waggled his eyebrows, pursed his lips, seemed to be trying to speak but nothing came out. Kate said politely:

'I really am an artist, Mrs Pratt. Vera Dan at the White Swan will vouch for me. I did her new inn sign.'

'I've seen it.' Mrs Pratt looked Kate over. 'You're strong anyway,' she said. 'Give me a hand with this and that and I don't mind feeding you. That Fred thinks I've nothing to do all day. What with him and his dad and the farm-hand to look after I've enough on my plate.'

Kate was a bit taken aback. No money *and* help out with the chores? But Fred's face was anguished and her heart ruled her head. There was, after all, something in Mrs Pratt's view of her position.

'I don't mind helping out. But only when I'm not working on the van. After all, that's what I've come to do.'

'The van,' Mrs Pratt sneered. 'How he's got the energy left for that nonsense I don't know. But come in girl, come in. Just so long as you and I understand one another.'

Kate followed Mrs Pratt's solid form into the house. A couple of clucking hens got in too. Fred, with a quick wink and a grimace dissolved away across the farmyard.

The kitchen seemed extremely full of things. A great scrubbed deal table, assorted chairs, buckets, saucepans, a cat in a basket, a rag rug, and a black iron range glowing with heat before which washing was airing. It was hot and steamy and smelled of starch and stew. Not at all like the delicate and delectable odours of Castle Café. But Kate liked it.

The stairs were very steep; the bedroom tiny and stuffed with strange objects. A broken suitcase stuck out from under the bed; a pile of old magazines lurked in one corner. But the view from the window across meadows to the moors was magnificent.

'It's not much,' said Mrs Pratt gloomily, 'but our Fred knows it's all we have. Take it or leave it. That old van can get along as it is for a bit longer yet.'

Kate tossed her backpack on to the many hued coverlet of crochet squares.

'It'll be fine, Mrs Pratt,' she said, 'and I do appreciate that you're very busy. I'll try not to be a trouble.'

'Huh!' said Mrs Pratt unbelievingly.

But presently they were seated at the kitchen table drinking large cups of strong tea. The two hens had been chased out and there was no sign of Fred.

'He's not a bad lad,' said Mrs Pratt with a sigh, 'but I wish he hadn't got this group bug. They all get it. Too much TV if you ask me.'

Kate was wondering where Fred and his mates practised. She had caught a glimpse of a neat parlour with many ornaments and a window-sill of potted plants. It was plain that his mother would never allow that sort of caper in there.

'You never know, Mrs Pratt. He may go on to fame and fortune!'

'We could do with a bit of that,' said Mrs Pratt morosely, 'but I doubt it. Best you can say is that it could be worse.'

'Perhaps he'll grow out of it?' suggested Kate. 'He's young yet.'

'There is that,' agreed his mother. 'We'll keep hoping.'

Fred came in, grubby from farm work. He washed thoroughly at the kitchen sink before joining them at the table. Cutting a large lump of bread and cheese he began to eat hungrily.

Mrs Pratt got up to get on with preparing supper.

'Now mind your manners, Fred,' she admonished.

Fred gave Kate a cheesy grin and said through a full mouth: 'Don't mind Ma. She's all right really.'

Mrs Pratt tossed her head and slammed some dishes about.

'Where do you practise, Fred?' asked Kate.

'Out there in the big barn. Ma won't have us in the house. There'd not be room, anyway.'

'Do you make up your own songs?'

'We try. We'll get better. But mostly we play what's popular. You know — stuff the kids can dance to.'

'How many of you are there?'

'Just the three. Ned on the drums, Jim and me on the guitar — and I'm the vocal.'

'You are?' said Kate, fascinated. She tried to imagine Fred, with his knobby face and sticky out ears warbling from a TV screen and came to the conclusion that he wouldn't look more peculiar than many.

Out in the yard the hens scattered and Fred pushed open the huge double doors of the wooden barn. Despite stored farm machinery and bales of straw stacked all round the walls there was plenty of space inside.

'That old straw, it sops up the sound like,' explained Fred.

The floor was of trampled earth, firm and dry.

'I reckon you can work in the yard as long as it keeps fine. Then rainy days I'll shift her in here.'

'That'll be okay' agreed Kate. 'Shall I go and get paint and stuff tomorrow? Do you know what colours and patterns you want?'

'Bright,' said Fred. 'Eye-catching. Advertising is what it is all about. I'll run you in to shop in the morning.'

How pleasantly different from Mr Stringer's reactions to her request to shop. Kate warmed to Fred. A man of no nonsense.

That night she lay in her narrow bed listening to the farmyard sounds which came in with the soft air of the summer night. Hens muttering as they settled to sleep; the stamp and clatter of the horse as he nosed his bucket; the croak of frogs from the duck-pond. Both the work and the surroundings were unquestionably new and different. Kate smiled to herself as she snuggled down to sleep. She ought to enjoy herself — she *was* enjoying herself — and yet, as her eyes closed and she drifted away, she knew a sense of loss.

# 16

Kate called the hens: 'coop — coop — coop' and clattered the ladle on the bucket. The hens ran from all directions as she flung out the corn mix. The cockerel stood, proud and protecting, calling a little, and watched his harem feed before tucking in himself. What a gentleman, thought Kate.

Why she should be helping around the place as well as painting the van and getting bare bed and board for her pains was a mystery. Well, not really. The bed and board belonged to Mrs Pratt and the van to Fred. It made a sort of sense. Kate liked Fred. She thought his mother quite capable of sending her packing and, after all, it *was* extra work for an already very busy lady.

Came the day when the van's new personality was complete. Kate was pleased with it. Just as she had imagined, splendid monsters' heads with horns and protruding eyes stuck up out of silver streaked green and blue water. She hoped that no-one would notice the rather close resemblance between Fred and the largest monster:it even had his wide melon-slice grin. Tucked into corners were small clusters of narrow boat roses.

Mrs Pratt and the boys stood around to admire. The group were really excited by their new image and even Fred's mother gave grudging approval.

'Though why you want to make a laughing-stock of yourselves all round the county I shall never know.'

'Oh, Ma,' protested Fred. 'We want to be the best of everything. Best group, best voice, best van.'

Mrs Pratt wiped her hands on her apron. 'That's as maybe,' she said gruffly, but she looked pleased. 'I suppose this means you'll be off again on your travels, young woman? Well — I have to admit you've done a good job *and* been quite handy to have around.'

'Why, thank you Mrs Pratt! I've enjoyed my stay and I do think the van has come out rather well.'

Mrs Pratt departed for the kitchen.

'Tell you what, Katey,' said Fred. 'You must come out on our first gig with her. A christening, like. How about it?'

'Great!' said Kate.

She fetched her washing from the line in the orchard, ironed it and hung it by the range to air. She settled for a bright shirt and fresh jeans for this was strictly a rural occasion. The boys piled a piano-accordion and a banjo into the back of the van as well as their usual gear.

'Doing Country and Western tonight,' explained Fred. Kate was invited to take the front seat next to the driver while Ned and Jim squashed into the back with their assorted instruments.

The van rocked and swayed as they bumped down back lanes for what seemed a very long time. At last they pulled up in a muddy field alongside a building that looked rather like a tram shed. At once a crowd gathered around chatting and joking about the bright decorations on the van.

'See you coming ten miles off down the valley!'

'What you got there — Loch Ness monsters?'

The boys grinned and cracked wittily back as they unloaded. They were pleased with the effect of their refurbished baby.

The space inside was very long with a high curved roof and bright flares of lighting from lanterns hung on the walls. It housed a collection of steam traction engines. The highly polished brass fittings on the splendid giants shone like old gold. They stood down one side roped off from the crowd, attended by slaves armed with oily rags and enthusiasm.

Halfway down the hall stood an old farm wagon and it was on this that the Canal Creatures set up their band. Kate watched. She still found it hard to believe that gangly Fred with his wide mouth and craggy face could produce anything that she would recognise as music. But she was wrong. The ballad into which the group swung was melodious and tender. And from that unlikely looking character that was Fred Pratt came a smooth, deep voice that twanged the heart-strings.

Kate stared. Fred even *looked* different. In his blue check shirt, open at the throat, a wide felt hat perched on the back of his head, his tanned face earnest with emotion, he looked the cowboy he was evidently feeling. The crowd cheered and applauded. Another ballad and the group broke into music for dancing.

Kate wandered along the line of massive engines admiring their air of power and the elegance of design necessary to produce that power. She chatted up the attendants, some of them elderly men who had driven these same machines in their youth.

The air was heavy with the smell of oil, sweat, and frying sausages. The doors at the end of the building had been left open so that one could see the starry sky. But despite this it was hot. There were stalls selling hamburgers and others selling soft drinks. Kate bought a hamburger in a bun wrapped in a paper napkin. It was liberally seasoned with relish and sliced onion. She also bought a tin of coke. With food in one hand and drink in the other she strolled down the long shed. The music was infectious and she would have liked to dance but, although some of the locals eyed her hopefully, it was obvious she could not take the floor until she had eaten her supper. However, Kate caught the looks and was cheered. It shouldn't be hard to get a whirl once her refreshments had been consumed.

One man spoke to her: 'Saw you come with the van. You'll be a friend of Fred's?'

'That's right.'

She smiled back at him. He looked doubtfully from her full hands to the dancers.

'See you later then.'

He looked nice.

Kate drifted on. At the far end of the hall was a bar. There were benches and tables and huge wooden kegs of beer. Also a counter from which stronger liquor was being served.

From this distance the music was slightly muted. Fred had gone back to a ballad, evidently a well-known one as other voices took up the refrain and soon a lot of people were singing along. Or perhaps shouting was nearer the mark! It was a cheerful sound. Kate paused, wondering if she should sit down while she finished her meal. She looked around for a space.

There was a fair-haired girl sitting staring down into her drink. She looked familiar. The girl looked up. Her face was pale and her eyes wide and blank. She tossed her head so that the blonde hair fell back from her forehead. It was — surely it was Margy? And yet the young woman sitting there had none of the relaxed and youthful charm that Kate remembered.

She picked up a small glass of clear liquid and tossed it back in one swallow. She said something to her companion and laughed with a kind of glittering gaiety. It *was* Margy. The voice, muffled though it was by the sound of the Canal Creatures belting it out at their best, was immediately familiar.

'Margy!' cried Kate. 'How lovely to see you!'

The girl turned and stared at her with a strange, hard expression. She got up, walked round the table and stood in front of Kate. Yes — it was Margy all right but so changed from the fresh-faced young woman that Kate remembered that it was hard to believe.

She said again: 'Margy?' but on a more doubtful note of interrogation.

The face in front of her changed, tensed, became a mask of hate. The eyes lost their blank look and seemed to shoot out sparks of fury. The slim fingers bunched to small fists and then opened and stretched.

'I know you,' she said. 'What are you doing here? Why are you following me? You took my man — isn't that enough?'

Startled, Kate stepped back, but with a cry that was almost a scream Margy sprang at her. In a moment she had both hands locked in Kate's red curls and was twisting viciously while, at the same time, she hacked at Kate's ankles with a foot.

Kate was helpless. She was unprepared. Both of her hands were occupied. The pain in her head made her eyes water and she feared her hair would be torn out by the roots. She dropped the half-eaten hamburger and the can of coke crashed to the floor making a sticky pool.

All at once they were surrounded by

people. The music had stopped. There was a hubbub of voices. Her head felt on fire. She put her hand up to her forehead; it came away sticky with blood. Margy's nails, as she had been forcibly disentangled from Kate, had slipped and gashed Kate's face. Fred was there looking concerned.

'No, Fred. I'm all right now. You must get on with your show.'

She mopped at her forehead with an already stained handkerchief.

Fred looked very worried.

'Sure?' He glared at Margy. 'I know her. See her around the clubs. Should be barred if you ask me.'

Someone led Kate to a bench and put a glass of cold lemonade in front of her.

'Thank you,' she said gratefully. She sipped and smiled and gradually people began to melt away. There was some feeling that Margy should be flung out but Kate stopped it.

'No. She's a friend of mine. Honestly.'

'A friend?' they said, astonished.

'She didn't know what she was doing. I'm sure she didn't.'

Shaking their heads and muttering they went away.

Margy sat with her head in her hands. After a while she looked up. Her face was still pale but the glare in her eyes had gone and she looked like Margy again.

'Kate! I'm sorry. It was the shock. I never expected to see you again. I'm afraid — I'm afraid I was quite out of myself for the moment.'

'Yes. I could tell,' said Kate drily. 'Do you do this sort of thing often?'

'Never — never,' said Margy eagerly. 'I've never gone off like that before, have I Dirk?'

Her companion had an arm around Margy's thin shoulders. He shook his head.

'No,' he said. 'It's my fault. I should look after her.'

'Well,' said Kate comfortingly. 'No harm done. Or not much. But you gave me a fright.'

And indeed, she felt trembly inside now that it was all over and wished very much that she was home in bed.

The great hall, which had seemed pleasantly unusual and attractive with its splendid machines gleaming in the soft light, had now faded to drabness. It was nothing but a corrugated iron shed, air stuffy with cigarette smoke and floor littered with bits of greasy paper and slippery with spilt drink.

'Anyway you're quite wrong, Margy,' she said. 'Roly finished with me years ago. Can't you understand that? We are truly just friends.'

The blue eyes were fixed on hers with a tragic expression.

'Then why doesn't he want me?'

'It isn't *that*,' said Kate despairingly. 'I can't explain how Roly's mind works. He's not like other people.'

'I know,' said Margy, and her voice was soft.

Kate looked at Dirk. It seemed very hard that Margy's escort had to listen to all this about another man. Dirk gave her a rueful grin.

'I'm used to it,' he said. 'And after all — I'm the one that's here! Don't worry. I'll get her home. I always do.'

Kate took the bunched handkerchief away from her head where she had been holding it to staunch the scratch.

'Oh!' Margy's eyes opened wide with horror. 'Did I do that? I'm so *sorry*, Kate.'

'Not to worry. It's all over now.'

'Will you — will you tell Roly?'

'How should I do that? I haven't seen him for ages.'

But she made no promises. Perhaps if Roly did know it would make him realise . . .

A tap on her shoulder made her look up. The friendly young man was back.

'How about a dance now, lass? If you're feeling up to it?'

All at once there was nothing Kate wanted to do more than dance. To lose herself in the music until her shaken self came together and she knew who she was again. She stood up and was pleased to find that she felt quite steady. Her new friend led her away.

'That's the ticket,' he said approvingly. 'Okay now? Right little hell-cat, your mate, ain't she?'

'She can be,' said Kate primly and they both laughed. And though her head still ached a little her feet moved deftly and the rest of the evening was fun.

Going home in the van the boys sang and Kate, half drowned in an old sweater of Fred's, drowsed, and watched the shadowy countryside slip by in the moving light.

Would she see Roly again? It seemed a very important question. She thought that she must.

# 17

Though the sky overhead was grey, Kate felt a lift of the heart as she stepped out on to the quay. Yes — the Rose Ann was at her moorings. It had begun to rain very gently, plopping into the water to make tiny circles. The boat looked deserted. But perhaps Roly was inside.

Kate stepped aboard and went down into the cabin. The bed was still pulled down and covered with rumpled blankets. It was warm and cosy amidst the decorative china and frilly mats. She yawned. The bed needed tidying. She straightened a blanket. Why not lie down for a moment?

A harsh rasping as of sandpaper on her cheek made her open her eyes. Two shining yellow lights were close to her face. For a moment she shrank back and then she remembered.

'Ailsa!' she cried and patted a furry cheek.

'Who's been sleeping in *my* bed?' came a deep bearlike voice.

Roly was standing over her with a grin on his face and a steaming mug of coffee in one hand.

'Hallo!' said Kate. 'I must have fallen asleep!'

'So you must,' agreed Roly, 'though what you are doing here at all is another matter!'

'I came to see you. You weren't here and I was very tired so . . . '

'I was walking Ailsa,' said Roly. 'Get up and I'll tidy up and then you can tell me why.'

He heard out her account of the meeting with Margy with a grave face.

'I know she's going the pace,' she said, 'but I didn't know it was that bad. What do you think it was? Drink or drugs?'

'Who can say?' She was sorry afterwards but just for a moment she was quite crazy.'

Roly frowned and chewed his lower lip.

'I don't know, Kate. I'm older than her, I've got no proper job, no prospects in my career. But if she's going on like this . . . Perhaps it would be better . . . But me? Look after somebody? I can't even look after myself!'

'I don't think that's the point, really. I expect Margy would do the looking after. But she needs somebody very badly and for some reason it seems to be you!'

Looking at Roly it might be hard for a stranger to see why a personable young woman would wish to throw herself at his head. His thick navy sweater was frayed at the cuffs and had holes in it. Today his long wispy brown hair had been roughly brushed and tied at the back of his head in an untidy cue. His face was rather lined and his eyes anxious. But Kate still remembered and knew that Roly, when he put himself out, had a great deal of that indefinable asset, charm. And also a very kind heart. The question was — did his determination to keep free of entanglement still endure?

'I shall have to think about it. I'm almost sure . . . But what about you, Kate?'

'I've got my problems too,' she said. 'The only job I have on offer at the moment is one from Giles Harcourt to paint his roses for a brochure for the gardens. I want to do it but I don't want to get involved and Giles . . . '

'Giles fancies you. And you fancy him. So what is the problem?'

Kate looked rueful.

'The same as yours, I guess. On the one hand I tell myself that as a freelance I can't turn down work. On the other hand I feel it's unfair to go back unless I have something to offer other than mere employability. He's sure to think there's more to it than that.'

'And is there?'

'I don't know. I really don't. I *like* being free, doing my own thing, being responsible for no-one but myself.'

'And you can really imagine feeling like that all your life? Sooner or later responsibility will find you out, like it or not. Better pick your own before you're landed with something you don't want.'

Kate looked thoughtful.

'That's one way of looking at it. But you remember, Roly, that what's sauce for the goose is sauce for the gander!'

'Enough of the philosophy! Tell me all about your travels!'

The cabin became warm and stuffy with the aroma of damp dog and hot coffee. Kate talked on, telling of Robert and Tamsin, Mr Stringer and Fred. Roly took a good view of Fred but shook his head over the Stringer episode.

'He sounds a right crooked customer, that one. I'm glad you didn't stay around Moor End Farm. I wonder why he asked if you could *copy* pictures? Something very odd there. I suspect he is in some illegal racket.'

266

'Yes. I think so too. I didn't really like him. And yet, in a way, I'm disappointed, because I've never before been offered a commission and not carried it out. I could have fixed the picture I was shown. And I'd only got the word of this lady, and instinct, to go on.'

'You were right,' said Roly firmly. 'It wasn't the sort of set-up in which you should get involved.'

They opened the cabin doors and let in the fresh air. Outside the clouds had cleared, blue sky showed and a little breeze had sprung up, rippling the water.

'I think you should take that job with Giles. He's old enough to look after himself. And you really want to do the work.'

'Yes, I do,' confessed Kate. 'Painting flowers is the thing I like best.'

'Go on. You do it.'

'Really, Roly? she said wistfully. 'It doesn't seem quite fair in a way . . . '

Roly looked at her.

'I thought you wanted to do your own thing? This *is* your own thing. You're not being free — not being true to yourself — if you turn it down over such tenuous scruples.'

Kate turned and looked out of the doors. Now the grey sky had gone everything seemed more hopeful and possible. Talking to Roly had been a great help. She had come (she thought) to tell him about Margy but he had helped her to make up her mind.

The walk up the hill towards Court Castle was pleasantly familiar. Kate felt her spirits life with anticipation. Soon she would see her friends again — soon she would see Giles. The white goat wandered over through the damp grass and trod heavily on her toes with its horny cloven feet. She rubbed the rough white head which butted against her and pushed the heavy hairy body away. The goat, affectionate but smelly, tramped after her up the path.

Pushing open the gate Kate climbed

the terrace between the trailing rambler roses. She reached the top to find a surprising number of cars parked on the semi-circular gravel forecourt. Among them was Rowenda's gold sports car.

Slightly dismayed — could they be giving a party? — Kate stepped cautiously up to the drawing-room windows and peeped in. There were certainly a great many people present, mostly standing, and with drinks in their hands. Tamsin was passing about with plates of small savouries. Giles, with Rowenda at his side, was talking animatedly to a group of several people. But it did not look like an ordinary cocktail party. For one thing those women present were not sufficiently smartly dressed. The gathering had a more work-a-day appearance. Glancing round at the cars she saw one with a sticker saying 'Press'. Looking back into the room she noticed a pile of papers on a table and that people were taking them away to read.

At that moment Giles glanced across

the room towards the window. His expression altered to one of astonishment which quickly changed to pleasure. He turned and said something to Rowenda and then disappeared.

Kate stepped back. He had seen her. Oh dear — it did not seem at all a suitable moment to be turning up.

She had moved away from the window and out of sight, she hoped, of the visitors.

Giles hurried towards her across the gravel drive.

'Kate!' he said eagerly. 'You've come back! Did you change your mind?'

He was looking particularly well turned out, his fair hair smooth and shining, even the unruly lock temporarily in place. Kate felt extremely shabby and a bit grubby.

'I'm sorry,' she said. 'I'm interrupting. I'm sure this is business, isn't it?'

'Yes. A Press party. To launch this season's brochure. But never mind that. Are you taking the job I offered you?'

She looked at him shyly.

'If you still want me to.'

His face lit up.

'Want you to? Of course I do! But now I have to get back. Come inside and meet the others.'

He held out his hand. Kate shrank back looking horrified.

'No, no! I'm a mess! I can't go in there!'

Giles laughed.

'Come on, Kate. This is not like you! What do you care for what people think?'

Kate hesitated.

'Come on. I want you to be there when I announce my new rose!'

'All right. But only if you'll let me get changed first. I *can't* mix with civilised people dressed like this. And I probably smell of goat! I had a lot of attention from Nancy on the way up the field!'

'OK. I'll see you later then.'

He gave her a happy grin and disappeared back into the house. Kate made her way round to a side door and then slipped up the stairs to the bathroom. In the bottom of her bag she kept an almost uncrushable dress for just such emergencies. She had a good wash then shook out the dress and slid it over her head. The silky fabric settled smoothly, outlining her bust. The low scooped neck revealed her creamy skin then flared out from a neat waist and swirled around her hips. The material had a faint sheen and the rich emerald green set off her red curls to perfection.

Kate looked at herself in the mirror. It was a long time since she had looked and felt so feminine. It was a nice feeling. She almost floated down the stairs towards the muted roar which stated that the party was a success.

As she crossed the small landing she saw that the picture of Giles' grandmother was back in its old place. Was the lady smiling at her? She seemed like an old friend.

The main door stood open to keep the house cool. A small man dressed for gardening and wheeling a barrow, paused just outside and peered in. Seeing Kate descending the stairs he moved away. This must be the extra help that Giles had taken on because Margy was so often away.

Kate went into the drawing room and paused just inside the door. Someone gave her a glass of sherry. She saw Mary smiling at her from across the room and Tamsin materialised at her side with her tray of canapes and an enthusiastic welcome.

The room was very full. Everyone was talking. Bowls of roses stood on the tables shedding coloured petals. Presently Giles called for silence. He made a short speech thanking everyone for coming and saying that he hoped they would find lots of interesting things in the brochure.

'For we've done our best to provide background stories and historical facts as well as details of the appearance and prices of our roses. Any publicity you can give us will be very welcome. As you know, we started in a small way of business but we have prospered and I believe we are set to become one of the great rose firms of the future.

'Now I want to announce my new rose of the year. A modern shrub rose, strong, robust and very free flowering. It will bloom intermittently throughout the summer. The flowers are not large and are borne on big open sprays. The outer petals are fiery red shading inwards to a heart of gold. It has a strong fragrance something like honey. I call it 'Sweet Kate of Court.'

There was a ripple of applause as Giles stopped speaking and he looked straight across the room at Kate. She was very pale and held her hands loosely clasped together before her breast. Her lips silently formed the words 'thank you' as their eyes locked across the room.

# 18

When Giles looked out of the window and saw Kate he thought at first that he was hallucinating. The room was crowded with local Press and representatives of gardening magazines. It must be just another late-comer that he was seeing. It could not be — it *could* not be — the vagabond artist who had come and gone through his life leaving it shaken and disturbed in a way he had never intended.

The figure drew back but not before he had realised, with a great lift of delight, that it was truly she.

From the time he collected Tamsin and had his offer of work rejected he tried to put Kate Trevine out of his mind. There was so much to do. The gardens were beginning to pay off. He was starting to get a reputation as a rose grower. Work had been everything to him for so long that he had not at first recognised the feelings growing in his heart. He had kept the company of women strictly for relaxation and entertainment and never let his vision of one — not even the delectable Rowenda — get in front of the important things in life.

By the time he realised that here was someone who had quietly taken possession he also realised that he had left it too late. She had escaped back to the world from which she had come. A freewheeling world without obligations, without restriction, without personal commitment.

But she was here. He made his way quickly through the throng. She seemed diffident and unsure. He was totally intent on keeping her now she had, so unexpectedly, reappeared.

Returning to the party he wondered — had he been abrupt, too businesslike? At least she had agreed to stay. When she entered the room, looking light and elegant in the green dress, it seemed to

Giles as though there was a glow in the air around her. Across the room he offered her his gift — his rose — and saw that she understood.

The party broke up. The cars roared away. Amidst the litter of empty glasses and plates Mary and Tamsin rushed up to Kate, pleased and excited to see her again. Rowenda was the last to go. Giles escorted her out to her car.

'Tell us *everything* that has happened to you since we last saw you!' cried Tamsin.

'That would take a very long time!' laughed Kate, wondering how much of her strange adventures were suitable for the telling.

Especially she wondered about the incident with Margy. Roly had that in hand, she hoped. A quick look round had shown that Margy, as so often, was not at home. Not even a party had been enough to keep her there. Best to say nothing.

'That went well, Giles,' said his

mother, when he came back into the room.

'Yes,' said Giles. 'I think so. Goodness, what a mess!'

'We'll soon straighten things up,' said Mary.

'Yes,' said Kate, relieved to have something to do. 'Lend me an apron and I'll get stuck in.'

Giles looked as though he was going to say something but thought better of it.

'Come on Giles,' sang out Tamsin. 'Many hands make light work!'

Groaning a little, Giles complied.

Sometime later the drawing-room was back to its usual comfortable state: the floor swept, the tables cleared, the cushions plumped. Mary and Tamsin were stacking dishes in the kitchen. Kate looked round and sighed with satisfaction. It was the most pleasantly restful room she had ever known.

For a moment Kate thought she was alone. She untied her apron and ran her fingers through her curls. But

Giles was there. His hands were on her shoulders as he gently turned her towards him. The blue eyes looking down at her were so warm and gentle that her heart melted and she felt slightly giddy.

'I ought — to go and help the others,' she said nervously.

'Don't run away again,' said Giles. 'I don't think I could bear it.'

She looked up at him resolutely, knowing that she must get this over quickly.

'I've come to work. I'm taking the job you offered me. To paint roses for your next brochure.'

'Of course you have,' he said tenderly. 'So let's go out and look at some roses, shall we?'

'What now?'

'Why not?' She could not think of a reason except that she feared to be alone with him and that she could not say so she walked docilely by his side. As they came down the steps the small man she had seen peering in the door went by, touching his cap to Giles as he passed.

'Is that your new garden help? He was looking in the door when I came downstairs. For you, perhaps?'

'He's an odd fellow. Always peeping in the windows. But he's useful. Just odd jobbing. I take him on for a week at a time. Where did you spring from?'

'Immediately — from the Rose Ann. I went to see Roly.'

'Ah.'

She saw his face stiffen.

Kate stopped and stamped her foot.

'Don't be so silly, Giles! Roly was my boy-friend at art college but our relationship went cold — cold — cold — years and years ago! Now he's my friend — he understands me.' She added hastily and in some confusion: 'Not that its any of your business.'

White roses tumbled down the walls. White butterflies flickered over heavily blooming lavender borders. White pigeons strutted and cooed. They were out of sight of the house.

He stopped suddenly and caught her by both hands.

'Kate — don't play games. You know I love you. I've been desolate since you went away. You've come back. Tell me — does that mean you feel the bond between us too?'

She tried to pull her hands away but he was very strong and gripped firmly, the warmth from him entering her palms, surging up her arms and generating heat through her whole body.

'Please don't, Giles. You've got to understand. I don't want to be tied down. I want to be free.'

'I said that I love you. I didn't say that I wanted to tie you down.'

'Don't you see? If I let myself care for you deeply — as I could — I should be tied. I should be vulnerable — have given a hostage to fortune. I should have taken on responsibility, like it or not.'

He frowned down at her, trying to understand.

'I think you've got it all wrong. You can't run from love for ever.'

She recovered her hands and moved away, rubbing the back of her wrists. What was it Roly had said: 'Sooner or later responsibility will find you out.'

Giles said quickly: 'Did I hurt you? I'm sorry, I did not mean to. Let's walk on.'

He retrieved one of her hands and led her forwards. They stepped through the arch in the Leylandii hedge where Tamsin had lain and sobbed out her teenage woes. The sun, lower now in the sky, threw long blue shadows across the rose fields. The air was heavy with the scent of flowers.

He turned her towards him and stood looking down then pulled her into his arms. She felt his body holding hers tightly and his cheek resting on her hair.

'Look at me, Kate.'

She looked up and was lost.

Everything about this man called out to her: His scent, his strength, his smile, a kind of radiating warmth of personality. She put up a hand and pushed back the straying lock from his forehead as she had so often wished to do. He bent to kiss her and her fingers locked at the back of his neck. It was a long, hard kiss and it seemed to dispel all her doubts and reservations like the sun dissolving a morning mist.

Somewhere at the back of her mind her old life of freedom still beckoned; roads wound through fields and over mountains, leading to adventure and things unknown; the pleasures of being alone, beholden only to oneself, choosing the next move with no need to consult another's inclination.

There was fear lurking there also. Fear of becoming so bound to another that to be wrenched apart would be like a tearing of the flesh.

But wasn't that what adventure was all about? Setting forth bravely into a new country with a new companion and facing what the future might bring?

Slowly the world righted itself, bringing

back the sounds of buzzing bees, cooing pigeons, and a thin rustle of leaves from a rising breeze.

'Will you marry me, Kate?'

Her heart was banging so hard that she thought she would choke. She should not have come back . . . it was all too difficult. But she had come back of her own free will and deep inside herself she had known . . .

'I can't think — I don't know — '

He moved suddenly and she shrank back.

'No. Don't be afraid. I won't kiss you again. You are right. I'm just not very good at picking my moments, am I? Sleep on it, my darling. There's all the time in the world.'

# 19

The moon dived in and out of the clouds, making racing shadows across the field. Inside the shed the white goat lifted her head. She could hear a strange sound; she was curious. She pushed her forehead against the door. The sound grew louder; the goat pushed harder. The old wooden catch gave way and she was out.

Roly weaved his way up the path. He was very drunk. He sang as he came, a song which seemed suitable, a version of the Lincolnshire Poacher: 'Oh, it's my delight on a shiny night in the season of the year!'

Behind him slunk Ailsa. She knew very well that she should be guarding the boat, now tethered once more in the small landing bay at the foot of the hill, but her master hadn't ordered her to stay. So, feeling vaguely guilty, she followed him. Roly had one idea fixed in his head: he must find Margy; Margy needed him.

The white goat trotted across the sometimes silver grass and regarded him with interest. Roly's voice rose louder: 'Oh, it's my delight on a shiny night . . . ' The goat came alongside and butted him with her solid bony head. Ailsa growled. The goat ignored her.

Roly came to the small iron gate and managed to get it open. He went through. The goat followed; so did Ailsa. The odd procession proceeded to mount the terraces. The goat leaned on Roly in a friendly manner. They were almost at the top. She found it all very interesting. Roly caught his leg on a trailing thorny briar. Roly fell with a shout.

He lay on his back looking at the shifting moon while he swore loudly. It seemed too much effort to get up. The goat nosed at him. Maddened and alarmed Ailsa pranced and whined.

She planted her legs apart and barked her disapproval. She knew better than to attack this fur-coated, four-legged interloper. Training was stronger than instinct. All at once she sat down on her haunches and, lifting her muzzle towards the glimpses of moon, howled long and melancholy like her wolf ancestors.

Kate woke. She had lain for a long time trying to calm tumultuous emotions and sort out her thoughts until at last she had fallen uneasily asleep. Startled, she sat up. Something was wrong. What eerie noise was that? She grabbed her dressing gown and ran barefoot down the stairs.

On the half-landing she paused. She switched on the lights. The door of the drawing-room stood open. There was a man by the main entrance in the hall. He was dressed in a dark tracksuit and the lower part of his face was covered by a scarf. He turned. Something small and metallic gleamed in his right hand.

'No, no,' said Kate's common-sense self, 'that can't be a gun.'

But she knew that it was.

Something struck her heavily on one shoulder so that she fell sideways on to her knees. Someone sprang past her down the rest of the stairs. There was a report — not at all loud — and something zipped by her head and thudded into the lower part of the calm lady's picture.

Giles was down there wrestling with the uninvited visitor. They swayed to and fro as the stranger tried to get out of the house. In the struggle his mask slipped and Kate found herself looking straight into the eyes of John Stringer.

In that moment several things became clear. So this was how he collected pictures! From a long way back came the memory of the two men at the White Swan asking about Court Castle. A tall man and a short man. John Stringer and the inquisitive part-time gardener. But most of all, burning like fire, came the flash of fear as Giles catapulted past her and the bullet hummed.

All at once her desire for solitude, for pleasing only herself, her fear of involvement, seemed petty, selfish and unimportant. If Giles had been hit she would have suffered the pain in her own body; if Giles had died something in her would have died too.

It was over. The man had gone with Giles after him. The heavy outside door banged shut. Kate stood up and began to walk downstairs.

Outside the moon showed itself and shone down on Roly, lying supine among the ramblers while the white goat meditatively chewed his beard. Ailsa was still leaping up and down and creating a great deal of noise. Every light in the house was on.

Giles stood in the forecourt, panting and dishevelled, staring around. From the distance came the sound of a car starting up, quickly superseded by the roar of an approaching motor-bike.

Dirk drew his huge machine to a halt in a spurt of gravel. Margy climbed off the pillion and removed her helmet, shaking out her hair so that moonlight shimmered over glitter dust.

'Whatever's going on?' she asked.

Ailsa danced and howled with thwarted rage. Margy strolled to the balustrade and looked over. Roly, still lying on his back, looked up at her with a happy smile.

'Margy!' he articulated with some difficulty. 'I've come — I've come — to look after you!'

Tenacious thorns clung to his hair so that he seemed to have stuck a dozen small roses on the top of his head.

Ailsa, maddened to a frenzy, had been making little runs at the goat, not quite daring to nip her hind quarters. As Margy gazed down instinct came uppermost and the dog's small sharp front teeth met in the goat's backside. Though the most that the bite achieved was a mouthful of hair the goat jerked up her head to stare reproachfully round. A wisp of Roly's beard went too and he let out a yell.

Margy shrieked with laughter. She jumped over the parapet and knelt by his side, tenderly freeing him from the encroaching briars. Roly sat up and opened his arms and Margy cuddled into them. The goat, bored, drifted away and Ailsa, feeling that she had done her duty by her master sat and panted gently, grinning a doggy grin.

Up above Giles said: 'Did anyone see a car?'

'I did,' said Dirk. The moonlight picked out the shiny studs on his black leather jacket and glinted off the solitary earring which swung in his ear.

'Notice the number?'

'Sorry,' said Dirk. He was staring down at the affecting tableau below. 'So that's the way the cookie crumbles,' he said with resignation. 'Ah well — easy come; easy go.' He shrugged his shoulders and climbed back on his bike.

'Thanks for bringing my sister home.'

'A pleasure. So long.'

The bike leapt loudly back into life and Dirk was gone.

Leaving the unusual lovers encamped on the terrace, Giles went back into the house.

Kate entered the drawing-room and looked round. As she had expected the silver ornaments were still in their places on the marble mantleshelf but where the Victorian landscapes had hung there were only light patches on the wall paper. But the pictures had not gone. They had been placed on the floor, leaning against the wall, all but one small one which lay a little apart. It must have been the last one that John Stringer had handled.

Kate knelt down to examine the pictures. They did not seem to have been damaged yet, although they would almost certainly have suffered when stuffed into the black plastic bags which were piled nearby.

A noise made Kate look round.

Tamsin stood in the doorway wearing Donald Duck pyjamas; Mary beside her in a pink candlewick dressing gown.

'Has everyone gone mad?' demanded Mary. 'Barks and yells and motor-bikes and the whole house awake? After such a busy day I need my sleep!'

'Is it burglars?' asked Tamsin with interest. 'What fun!'

Giles loomed over them to see Kate kneeling on the floor with the small picture in her hands. She smiled up at him and he knew without telling that she had made up her mind. There was no longer anxiety, strain and doubt. There was only trust and love and thankfulness. But all she said was:

'This is valuable. Did you know? Your great-grandfather must have been a collector. One by this artist went for £20,000 at Sotheby's recently. I haven't had time to look at the others but if there are any more . . . '

'Never mind that,' Giles came into the room, 'are you all right?'

'Yes. But I'm afraid your grandmother

may have sustained some damage.'

Giles was looking down at her with a hungry expression. In front of all these people — surely he could not? But he did. She felt the all-too-ready blush rising to her cheeks. Bending, he swept her up and into his arms, then kissed her with ruthless thoroughness. When eventually he let her draw breath he remarked: 'What a good thing I'm going to marry a picture restorer.'

'Are you?'

He kissed her again. Kate came up gasping.

'Yes — oh yes — you are!'

There was laughter and applause from the interested watchers in the doorway.

Margy came in leading a rumpled but seraphic Roly.

'Can we live on the narrow boat, Giles, while Roly is looking for work? He's agreed to let me make an honest man of him!'

'No — sorry — Kate and I are taking the Rose Ann on our honeymoon. Why are you looking at me like that? Don't you think I can run her without Roly? But you will be with me, my darling — and together we can do anything!'

# THE END